Vilnius Diary

Old Europe.   Vilnius is just recovering from Soviet occupation.   A scientist travels to the country of his parents and digs into the stories and numbers of the Holocaust and Gulag.   His personal world begins to fall apart.   Things happen that he cannot explain.   Someone is leaving strange drawings in his apartment. Why?

Vilnius Diary

A novel by Ruta Sevo

with art by TaDas Gutauskas

print ISBN 978-0-9831588-3-7

Photo reproductions of paintings by permission of
Tadas Gutauskas www.tadasgutauskas.lt

Cover design and photo preparation by
Holly Russell www.hrphotographics.com

Photo of "moss" by permission of Jeffrey S. Milstein
Photo of "Julia" by permission of Audra Kauspediene
Photo of "Nisse" by permission of Holly Russell Milstein

Copies may be purchased at stores.lulu.com/sevo

From: Mingen, Zenius [zen@ulink.net]
Sent: June 30, 2003
To: 'semea@doos.com'
Subject: made it!

Semea –

I have met the motherland and it looks like it is going to be a one-sided date, with me doing all the work. Every Joe in the street speaks our private family language. I am not a stranger here, in looks or in language. The people in the street cannot tell that I have never been here before.

Of course, they don't think of their city in guide-book terms. In my mind, I collapse centuries of history and politics. It is the Jerusalem of the East, the center of a pagan land, a capital of a Catholic Poland, Soviet occupied, Nazi cleansed, a flourishing center of art and hope in the new EU, an inexpensive tourist destination, and the home where our parents fell in love. I find it odd to feel a pedestrian atmosphere. Instead of dramatic swells of tragic and wailing opera, it sounds normal and quiet. People are getting groceries and going to work. At the same time the streets are marked by broken stone walls, remnants of inscriptions, architectural flourishes of seven centuries and the detritus of maybe 35 generations of people like me. A German street name. Hebrew lettering on a gate. A grimacing Baroque statue just above street level. Russian greetings in the street. Polish grave sites. A modern art studio showing bizarre, unwearable clothes. An Internet café in a windowless tiny catacomb of a room right off a narrow cobblestone sidewalk. I could read the screen as I passed by. A small patch of earth in the middle of a dense street with grass overgrowing some memorial marker. The Austrian Embassy residing in a building identified as the former synagogue in the ghetto. The U.S. Embassy in buildings that once housed the Soviet occupiers. Beautiful 13th Century streets that were also 20th Century killing fields.

I am still busy with the logistics of settling in. Getting used to walking everywhere. Hauling groceries.

My arrival at the lab was met with curiosity and gratitude. They are hungry for resources, and for people who know what's being done in the rest of the world. I feel like this is going to take me away from feeling

1

stuck in a rut in Portland. Get me outside myself, for a long time. Like reading an enormous good book.

The place is quite modernized. I've spent hours in a K-Mart like store, partly touring the goods. They have a deli with carry-out beet soup, herring, and fried chicken. Anything that costs more that $3 seems pricey. $3 can get you clothes, lunch. Milk and eggs are about 50 cents, as is most fruit.

The average salary is $6,000 per year, and pensions are $150 per month. Somehow, you buy a place to live for $30,000-60,000, and then all you have to cover is food, clothing, and gasoline. You can eat for $1.50 frugally. I've been having lunch in a restaurant for $3, and dinner with wine for $5. The big challenge for the residents is getting the place to live.

One of my colleagues introduced me to a painter in his 30's. He had to drive home to pick something up and invited me to come with him. He and his wife built a beautiful house in the "suburbs." It was wooded, with unplanned dirt roads between houses & little farms. It is about 10 miles from the town center. It has 12-foot high ceilings, huge single-pane windows on all sides, blond wood floors, three bedrooms, an aluminum-faced stove, and a very tall and metallic fridge as good as you can get in the U.S. Minimally furnished though. Their big purchases depend on the barter of a painting, or the sale of a painting. After a good show in Amsterdam, they bought 2 used cars. I have no idea what they did before that, for transport, because it is the dickens out of town, like a country home. They built it with help from parents, and from the sale of an in-town apartment that appreciated nicely. Still, $60,000 for a custom house that would cost $250,000 far out in the Seattle suburbs. It costs $3 to have the lawn mowed. Their ample yard is nothing but brick in front with two giant, old, apple-laden trees, and nothing but deck, soft grass, and three giant, old apple trees in back. The trees are part of an orchard that got invaded by houses. The trees set such an atmosphere, like paintings. There are red-cheeked apples fallen everywhere on the ground, as if they were an artist's standard yard decoration.

Had some food shocks. Kids like pizza with a ton of ketchup smeared all over the top. Ketchup regular or "Mexican ketchup." Green salad with chicken livers that look like little pieces of brain. All the meats seem fatty. After starving for a few days (jet lag, lack of sense) I settled on staples of eggs, peanut butter, and yoghurt. Carried out a meal from a restaurant, which is where people like me are supposed to eat, and tossed most of it out because it was grizzly meat. Granted, I have not gone to good restaurants. They might cost $10! Also, there are about 30 kinds of milk; 10 different Kefir milks alone. Thirty kinds of coffee.

Food portions are really small, and that might explain the low cost too: a small soup or salad for $1. Someone told me that eating micro-waved food is bad for you. If you eat micro-waved food, your body gets micro-waved. You can get tons of fresh mushrooms, fresh berries, and fresh bread. Food is left out without covering it, open to flies.

I do have to walk to work. Fifteen minutes down a hill and 20 minutes back up. On the way: a casino, an internet café, a few clothing stores, the national literary archives, a night club with sex shows, and an antiques store. I am working in an 18th century monastery. Behind a 13th century church. The monastery part got destroyed and had to be rebuilt.

Oh yes, the lab helped me find an apartment. It is located in the compound of an old church. I think monks lived here too. Both Catholic and Jewish scholars over time. One bedroom, a sitting/living room, and a small kitchen. To get to it, I go up a very popular tourist street from the center of the old town, which is fairly small, and then duck through a few stone arches into a courtyard with the remains of a church in the center. There, it is stone quiet, with some greenery, surrounded by painted walls. Everything is muted yellow. In one of the surrounding buildings is my apartment. When I go in, it feels as if I disappear into the architecture, like a ghost. I wonder who else lives here, and if I will ever seen anyone. I don't hear anyone, or the street.

Well that's plenty of news for now! Hope all is well with you –
Your brother Zen

Attachment: oldcitystreet.jpg

From: Mingen, Semea [semea@doos.com]
Sent: July 5, 2003
To: 'zen@ulink.net'
Subject: Re: made it!

Zenius –

      I am glad to hear that you arrived safely. I guess I have some strange notions about former Soviet countries and worried that you would find chaos-crime- pollution- poverty- and-bitterness. You did not mention too much about people, except for the painter. Are you making some friends? Do you think you could, even with the language barrier?

      I went to the Hoh Rain Forest on the Peninsula for a moss tour. Can't get enough moss! My gardening club decided it was worth the five hour drive. We were tired when we got there, mid afternoon, but walked for a few hours before it got dark in the forest. It was like heaven! I could see creatures in spirit playing in the ferns and rocks at the feet of giant trees.

I don't remember you taking any trips to Hoh or to the peninsula. The rain forests stretch from Oregon to Alaska. They have to get more than 12 feet of rain every year to make them. Inside a rain forest, it never freezes, or gets hotter than 80 degrees. There are plants called epiphytes that never touch the ground! They grow on other plants, but they are not parasites. ("Let me rest my roots on your bark... I'll make you pretty.") There are hundreds of different mosses. Sometimes the trees insert roots into the moss to share the water they hold. When it is too dry for them, the mosses go dormant. When it rains, they wake up again.

I would like to invent a color for wool called "moss and epiphyte." What do you picture is the color of chaos-crime- pollution- poverty-and-bitterness?

Maybe epiphytes are plant cousins of the fairies. Rhymes with acolyte.

I put some more sword ferns in, down the hill in back. Too impatient to wait for a few to propagate. I am greedy for their lush fullness. I had quite a time getting down the hill and back up because it stays muddy so much of the time. I slipped and fell on my backside and slid down about thirty feet. Got my clothes, face, and hands muddied good. You would have laughed to see me that close to nature!

Take care of yourself, and let me know more about this adventure of yours –

Semea

Attachment: hohpic.jpg

From: Mingen, Zenius [zen@ulink.net]
Sent: July 9, 2003
To: 'semea@doos.com'
Subject: fever

Semea –

I met more people in the lab now. They are curious about an American joining their work here. They seem to think that all the exciting science is happening in America or in Europe, and they are behind. Seemed amused to hear that their small country has AIDS and TB strains that are unique and interesting to us foreigners.

One problem with socializing is that people smoke like fiends everywhere I've been. The transfer at the airport in Vienna was like a stage set on Broadway. Small, darkish lower level room like a bus depot. Gates on all sides, with exotic names: Poznan, Prague, Sofia, Budapest, St. Petersburg, Vilnius, Warsaw, Ankara, Yubljana, Tbilisi, Oddessa, Krasnodar. In the middle was a 10 x 10 canopy, and under it rails, the kind you tie horses too. Here, the smokers stood leaning on the rails. Their smoke, of course, went out from this central stage. A mother with her toddler on her hip, taking a puff. It seemed humiliating to have to stand in the center of the waiting room. Lots of puffs in restaurants too. A number of people are smoking through our lunches. Hard to get away from it. I am literally picking up the atmosphere!

People are also trying to learn English like mad. Did you know that some of our science grants that will pay for foreign partners require them to have a good command of English? What if we all had to learn Lithuanian, or Serbo-Croatian? One lab mate's little girl is learning Russian, English, Hebrew, and Spanish, and she is 11 years old.

What am I doing here? The big grant we got from NIH covers many dimensions of HIV/AIDS, and I am to look at the new drug-resistant TB to see what's up with it.

Speaking of scary diseases, I got a terrible fever last Sunday. The word "dengue" comes to mind. Sudden & severe, all night. Thought my brains might fry. Probably due to exposure to a virus new to me. The Western doctor I visited suggested I take a shower when I come back from the K-mart place because of the exposure to all those people. My colleague Jurava said, put some hot water & salt ("Salt – you know what I am saying – do you have any SALT?") in a bucket, as hot as you can stand, and soak your feet. Cures everything for her.

It helps to speak some Lithuanian because we are all switching languages constantly. The true blue Americans that I've met have learned the language, some from a spouse. Many web sites have the option to switch languages. Still, I had to read the label on my drugs in Lithuanian. Really stretching the "kitchen language" we learned at home.

Well, I am picturing you lying in the mud with your ferns. You always were up to your ears in whatever. I recall you were covered with flour every time you baked at home.
Take care, Zen

Attachment: monkhome.jpg

From: Mingen, Semea [semea@doos.com]
Sent: July 12, 2003
To: 'zen@ulink.net'
Subject: Re: fever

Zen –

    I hope you are well again. It is scary to think of you sick and alone there. Can you get proper medical care? I heard that some Russian medicines would not pass our standards. I would go for the salt water, myself.

    I sure don't like the part about smoking everywhere! Maybe you should wear a surgical mask like they do in Japan during flu season. That will make you an interesting foreigner! Just don't tell them you are American then, for our sake.

Have you been inside any old churches? I imagine they are extraordinary.

Ferns to you – Semea

From: Mingen, Zenius [zen@ulink.net]
Sent: July 14, 2003
To: 'semea@doos.com'
Subject: a summer night party

Semea –

Jurava, Malke and I drove "up north" to the sea (at least the inlet). It took four hours with a food break, crossing most of the country. There was a highway most of the way, with 2 lanes, divided. Police ready to pounce. Oncoming cars flashing a warning. Big difference: light traffic. The only adventurous part was coming back, on a 2-lane road. In the middle of the small town the road was blocked for construction. There was an interesting sign:

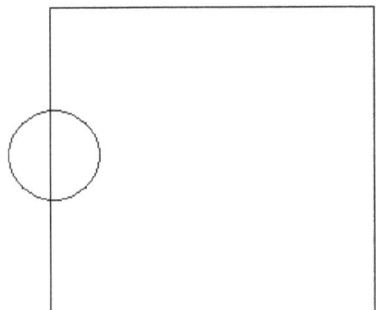

This meant detour. We drove to the right. Then suddenly the paved road just turned into a dirt road into the woods. Then it got overgrown, grassy, wild, with trees hugging it. This just after getting off the paved road. It was disappearing! Then muddy puddles in the road and deep muddy ruts showing that cars had barely made it through. It went on and on into woods. No turning back! Nobody in sight. No signs. We were in the middle of the woods, on a path barely wide enough for a car, seeming to turn into a foot path! Finally, a car full of people we knew caught up behind us. We were not alone. There was a branch in the narrow, muddy road. A horse and cart was coming towards us. We pulled over to the grass and asked about this detour. He said, yes, keep going. After about 2 miles of this, including crossing a potato field, we came out of the rough wilderness into view of a highway, with cars cruising along?? On the highway again, we passed very large oncoming trucks, and I wondered just how they handled that potato field?

We went to an arts festival. About 10 artists, including Finns and a Norwegian, had spent 10 days, each one building an outdoor sculpture on a grassy "park" beside an inlet. It was very pretty. The sculptures were all big carved wood pieces. We arrived for an auction of art. There were about 50 people squeezing in and out of a small restaurant + deck. The auction was fun although not many were bidding. The prices were 500-800 Litas ($200-300). The painter I know sold a painting to the Danish Ambassador who follows his work.

The setting was like a Bergman movie. A bunch of people disappeared, and it turned out they had gone for a boat ride. We hung around on the big deck. The missing people came back, and clustered & reclustered and starting drinking and eating, and continued for the next 6 hours. We sat at a few tables at the end of the lawn near the water. Spectacular sunset. Long grasses waving along the shore. Laughter from the restaurant hundreds of feet away, but close enough so that people could bring down more wine, beer and cheese. Word was "there is going to be a fish" to eat. People kept disappearing and reappearing. Apparently some personal dramas developed during the "camp." There were lovers; there were grudges. A cluster of old friends laughing at in-jokes (which I missed half the time).

The drinking escalated from wine to sweet liquors to straight vodka. We ate a fantastic Lithuanian farmer's cheese which is made by draining & squeezing all the juice out of dry cottage cheese. Consistency of mozzarella. Sliced, with olives & pickles on the side. Eaten in thick ½ inch slices. Later, "the fish" showed up. It was not dinner. It was a big white fish that had been smoking for hours that night, cut up into big 4-inch sections. Eaten with the hands. It tasted like smoked white fish. Maybe that's what it was. Salty. Certainly fueled some more drinking.

If I drank as much as a few of the people there, I'd be dead. They invited me to join a group heading for the sauna. I was not as "happy" as they were. Think: half quart of vodka. I went back to my rustic cabin for a sweater and fell asleep. After what seemed like one a.m. a bunch of naked people ran around in the dark outside, and were switching themselves or each other with branches. I was inside a tiny cold neat Ikea-like room with little wood cots & little wood chairs, no water/plumbing. The toilet was outside, a hundred feet away.

Of course, everyone was interesting to me. Architects. A man who made a fortune selling batteries, bought an old estate, and was remodeling it to replicate an authentic pre-Soviet era estate. There was a big debate about selling your personal house and whether you should advertise it, as if selling your home were somehow dishonest and shameful. People didn't used to buy and sell their houses. They got one and stayed to live and die through several generations in the same place. Best, Zen

Attachment: sunsetparty.jpg

From: Mingen, Semea [semea@doos.com]
Sent: July 19, 2003
To: 'zen@ulink.net'
Subject: Re: a summer night party

Zen –

I went to a bonsai show on the weekend. I am torn about "taming" nature, especially severely taming nature for my pleasure. I am trying to imagine this from the plant's point of view. If you were a tree, would you like being put on a pedestal and trained to look fabulous and like a miniature landscape? I guess ballerinas "torture" their natural and comfortable bodies into the unnatural states of being skinny, light, and walking on the tips of toes. Acrobats likewise, for our amusement. Using your body for art. Maybe these plants have chosen this path, and are eager for refined and sensitive masters who rewire their limbs to direct them into artistic poses.

No wonder I like moss. It is fuzzy, sloppy, hanging every which way, inviting, and pretty. "Touch me. I show you a SOFT world." – S.

From: Mingen, Zenius [zen@ulink.net]
Sent: July 22, 2003
To: 'semea@doos.com'
Subject: EU

Semea –

When you talk about nice nature I can't help think about the not-so-nice nature that I am working with. I am seeing what diseases can do to lives and don't see anything redeeming about it. I don't think people choose the path of a disease or death. It is nature's way of weeding, and sometimes it is totally random. Why did I get a fever some weeks ago? Bad luck. Didn't have immunity to the thing that bit me. Got exposed to the thing I didn't have immunity against. Folk beliefs – even modern "folk" – have it that people who get certain diseases deserve them. They used to think that about TB, and then cancer, and now HIV/AIDS. Must be our immature selves need to blame someone for misbehaving. "God's punishment." I see it more mechanistically – diseases are unearned, and certainly many are preventable. And some just come to us as mysterious time bombs, either spoiling or ruining our lives. Of course where they are preventable and we don't prevent them out of ignorance or lack of self discipline or self caring – that's stupidity and not bad luck. Then, I would agree that the disease is a punishment for bad behavior (but not necessary for bad morals).

On a lighter note. Here are tips on giving flowers, which you are supposed to do a lot in Lithuania: "Unless somebody has just died, make sure you give an odd number of flowers. One will do, but is not welcomed unless it's a single red rose for the one you love. Lilies and chrysanthemums are potent symbols of death and should be left well alone unless heading to the cemetery. If giving flowers to members of the older generations, avoid yellow ones. Yellow is the color of jealousy, and can be traced back to the Middle Ages when yellow was the traditional color of the dresses worn by ladies of a questionable profession. Carnations, especially red ones, are symbols of the communists. ...appropriate to give red tulips freely on International Women's Day.... Buy a bunch in the morning and dish them out..."

TV is frustrating. Every channel does a different suite of languages. Discovery Channel is dubbed in Russian. MTV was in German last night. Saw "The Last Emperor," which is Chinese people & setting, but an American movie. If you turn down the English so you catch just a bit here and there, what you hear is Russian (or Polish?) with Lithuanian subtitles. A lot of American programming. Horrible shows with people running around looking like" Polish Laugh-In." Lithuanian rap. The folkies from Klaipeda playing recorders, guitars, and violins. The two violinists were grim looking girls in folk costume. ("If you make me do this ONE MORE TIME...") BBC world going on about a soccer player. 15 minutes of BBC news. Almost 2 channels for every language, though: Lithuanian, Polish, German, Russian, and English.

Big changes coming with EU membership next year. Read a great "hey folks, get ready to change" published in the American Chamber of Commerce newsletter. The door to immigration will open, in a country that seems relatively homogeneous (for race) and isolated: nearly all white, Catholic. The linguistic mix is quite extreme, though. Competition

13

for jobs & new business when times are hard for most now. Brain drain, as the talented move freely about Europe, not needing visas and permits. Property values will rocket, as rich neighbors swoop in to invest. Move over, Lithuanian cheese. Start exporting those mushrooms. This is a country just getting over being invaded. Barely getting learning to compete, after the communists. They way that young people will leave when they are in the EU, but they will come back after 10-15 years, with a lot of experience. They say there will be higher quality media, because it will be owned by foreign capital.

I learned that tuition at the university is free. This is reassuring. Quality might suffer (low stakes education), but it's not the $100,000 differential between social classes that we have. A lot of people have managed to go abroad for a few years. Jurava's daughter goes to a small state-funded school specializing in Hebrew & Jewish studies. She had to have Jewish blood to gain entrance, thus the few students. There are fewer than 2000 Jews left in the country. The school has amenities like computers.

The Vilnius university bookstore has a low arched ceiling, completely painted like the Sistine Chapel. We would have turned it into a tourist shrine in no time. You shop for books, t-shirts and postcards, and then look up for a rush.

All for now – Z

Attachment: ubkstore.jpg

From: Mingen, Zenius [zen@ulink.net]
Sent: July 25, 2003
To: 'semea@doos.com'
Subject: bacteria

Semea –

I feel like I am eating bacteria three times a day. Kefir, Lactobacillus casei, acidophilus. The Swedes say the meat is the best in Europe. They don't eat liver in Sweden anymore, because it concentrates poisons, but here they think it is first rate. I do berries, myself. The nuts are not as good as Trader Joe's. Maybe after joining the European Union next year, Lithuania will be a mecca for food purists. "Come here to eat meat again."

Back to costs: Gasoline is the same here. Utilities are the same. Cars the same cost. The income is about 10 times less. Senior scientists make about $10,000 per year. And yet, stop in a country store and a bottle of water & ice cream together are 50 cents.

Since I am spending years on this virus, it has taken on a personality in my mind. I try to imagine it as a fellow creature in the struggle for survival. Like a cockroach, it has always been with us, insidious, and yet never something we have eradicated. We think in terms of preserving many species, but not all species. We also think in terms of eliminating certain diseases, and sometimes the carrier with it. Rats are still around even though the plague is not. Cockroaches are "innocent" carriers who like to be near our food and therefore act as a conduit for bacteria. It is not intentional. Even our pets can carry a bad agent.

HIV seems to thrive on ignorance and fears about sex. The ignorance seems to transcend all of our our modern cultures and societies. It seems independent of what we call civilization. Just because a society like ours has unbelievable media reaching every home through multiple television sets, telephones, home delivery of mail, brochures, universal education and literacy, it does not help us when we are about to engage in sex and we block on the potential dangers of exchanging bodily fluids. "I love you, therefore I cannot possibly be transmitting HIV in the act of love." "I hate you and will force myself on you, and therefore the fact that *you* may give *me* HIV is moot." "I don't know you but feel like having sex with you so let's not spoil it thinking of HIV." I wonder if there are societies – primitive? – where talking about sex was comfortable, and it could be discussed with the young, who have the strongest urges, and everyone could stay rational about some implications, and they would ALWAYS remember the danger and take precautions. Sex seems to trump fear.

I grow impatient hearing that whole countries are in denial about HIV. It is like a global family secret. Sex is taboo, a private matter, a holy matter between god and two people, or a shameful crime. Speaking about it is revolting or sinful. Dirty laundry, if you are a country. Authorities here are saying "We do not have this problem." As if to say "We are clean." In spite of facts that indicate they are *getting* the problem and rapidly. Yet watching people die of disease, leaving millions of orphans behind, is less revolting, or less sinful, or less immoral than talking about how people get the disease.   Our defenses include seeing these "infected people" as marginal – not normal, traditional, mainstream.   They are cast as dispensable, deserving, isolated or shunned. We do not let them interfere with our concept of our "normal" traditional family and society.

Of course I am surrounded by reminders of the massacre of Jews in Lithuania.   There are parallel questions: how can neighbors let neighbors die? How can neighbors help kill neighbors? What helps us so dissociate ourselves from people who are among us, and familiar, and possibly helpful and fun and friendly, to where we can watch them be pulled from their houses at dusk and loaded onto trucks. Do we roll over and go to sleep? Do we cower, feeling powerless? Are most of us so weak that we do not have the courage to think "we should use any means to fight the murderers, because this is wrong." "We should die fighting this affront to a civilized life."

Sorry to carry on. Long hours in the lab. Frustration. Slow progress.

Glad to have the relief of talking to you – Z

From: Mingen, Semea [semea@doos.com]
Sent: July 27, 2003
To: 'zen@ulink.net'
Subject: Re: bacteria

Zenius –

    Maybe your hours are too long. Take a walk!

    We drove up to Mount Rainier last weekend, and stayed in Paradise Lodge. It is at about 5,000 feet and above most the treeline, so the view is a sea of mountains and sky. Gary wanted to hike up to Camp Muir, at 10,000 feet. We did make it, but it took a steep trek up two miles of snow field to get there. It was like climbing an icy ladder into heaven. You would turn around and see Paradise Lodge get tiny, and the peer mountains – Adams, Hood, and St. Helens, get more prominent. Big ice fields dropping into steep ravines. People were spread out on the snow because there was no one trail. We saw each other on the hill for hours, stopping to rest, moving, stopping, looking. There was a man taking his little boy up. The boy must have been six years old and full of energy, following his dad wherever. He had no idea that he was doing a hike that few adults could do. Actually, he was probably better equipped for the climb than all the rest of us. He had no idea it was a big deal; walk right up. The rest of us were greedy for the high of being there. Gradually it got colder and chilly, a quiet index to the passage of time and increasing altitude.

    On the way down, the mists rolled in, hiding everything, including ravines and trails. As if the mountain were pushing us off – "I am covering up for the night, get lost." We almost did get lost, calling out in the thick fog. Some summer workers told us where to turn to get to the lodge. Otherwise, we could have gone downhill for ten miles and missed it.

S.

From:	Mingen, Zenius [zen@ulink.net]
Sent:	July 27, 2003
To:	'semea@doos.com'
Subject:	mushrooms

Semea –

I did take a walk. Went mushroom hunting with a small group organized by Jerry, who is here working in business development. His family is here too, and they try to take small excursions into Lithuanian life style. They are part of a of expatriates, who get together, and trade tips on where to find cheddar cheese or a barbecue grill, exchange American video tapes, and talk about how to keep their kids in touch with their real home in America.

We went mushrooming early Saturday morning. We drove out 2 hours toward Varena and met up with a Mushroom Master, who was discovered through various connections. He took us to one of his favorite forest spots and showed us the "number one, number two, number three" varieties of mushrooms. I snagged a few. He didn't waste his time pulling up any but the best variety. The forest is a bunch of straight, seemingly uniform evergreens, little underbrush, and deep up to 6" moss. The softest carpet. The mushrooms stick up their heads here and there. We were late for mushrooming (10 am). Late is a function of who got there first. There were "remains" of unwanted mushrooms strewn all over. It seemed wasteful, until I learned that mushrooms grow from one to five inches overnight, so you can go back to the same forest spot every day, and harvest them. And, even coming late, we found good ones. The ones that had been pulled up were being replaced as we watched. Found 2 poisonous varieties. A Lithuanian mushroomer had died the week before. Good to know where poisons are free for the picking, in case you ever need one. That makes a few natural poisons I know about personally -- learned of a poison fruit in St. John, Virgin Islands some years ago.

As you drive out of town, anywhere there is a forest next to the road, there are cars pulled over. Appearing to answer a "call of nature," which they are, if you consider the draw of mushroom hunting. Later in the morning, many have their baskets of mushrooms on display, for roadside sale. It seems a wonderfully plentiful crop, except that the nutritional value is not tremendous. I thought about the forest dwellers who lived in caves for years, avoiding the Soviets, and what free plentiful mushrooms could offer them. I gave away my lot of the #1 stuff, and learned later that my casual pile of loot might have been worth about $20.

The Debate about cooking mushrooms: The Mushroom Meister said boil them in water for at least an hour, and then you can cook them in food. If they are the "dark" variety, you have to change the water once. A bunch of us Americans looked at each other. I translated for us: "We just cut them up and sauté in butter." Oh. How strange.

By the way, I picked the right car pool. We drove out in an imported black Bronco listening to Barry White. There were tales from two people in the Foreign Service: expect to throw away a lot of food the first few months in a new location as you discover things you will not eat. That "gift trunk" of necessities like towels, cleansers, dishes, linen from the Embassy is not a gift. If you don't return every last fork, they come after you. Newbies to a location are assigned a "sponsor" who shows you, for example, how to pump gas and where to wash your car. They tend to you for a few months, or as long as necessary.

I went to an art show opening on Friday – "Vilnius and New York." Photographs. There were several hundred student-types packed into the art museum. Hari Krishnas dancing out front. Remember those? Felt like the 60's. They seemed to be the survivors of an ancient, nomadic tribe. Their chanting was much much better than I remember. Men and women standing apart from each other. Must have refined their culture, going backwards from modernity. Still, they looked like Americans in funny clothes. Inside, the crowds of young people were amazing. A wild array of hair styles, clothing styles. Men not afraid of long hair worn in many ways: pixie or Sikh, for example – little clump on top of the head. Women with various severe cuts, red dye. Statement-making clothes; student-cheap stuff. Most amazing was that men are not as conforming as those in U.S. The boundaries for "masculine" are far freer. There was a guy with baby-blue, hand-knit, sleeveless sweater, bare arms. He was with a babe, in case you think I got this wrong. I guess "bohemian" would describe much if this.

Outside, a ubiquitous type is the size-4 blond girl, who comes with a cell phone and a pack of cigarettes.   It's a skinny skinny lot. And tall. Everybody is smoking instead of eating, maybe.

See, I have gotten out of the lab.

Hope you are having sunshine in Seattle – Z.

Attachment: mushrooming.jpg

Attachment: countrychurch.jpg

From: Mingen, Semea [semea@doos.com]
Sent: August 1, 2003
To: 'zen@ulink.net'
Subject: Re: mushrooms

Zenius –
    We haven't seen any sun in weeks now. But the orchids in my little greenhouse box have sent out several new tendrils. It is thrilling to watch them reach out in an act of exquisite creation. They take their time, and unfold slowly, like a butterfly coming out of a cocoon, forcing open a protective bud to make room for what seem to be a crowd of more fragile petals. The petals breathe air and open as if they had reached nirvana. Blissful, quiet, kissing any light. Like a parachute that's been a small package sending out huge, thin membranes of color, of surprising volume.
    I have to run off to my Spirit Group meeting.
    Have you found any good souvenirs? Semea

From: Mingen, Zenius [zen@ulink.net]
Sent: August 15, 2003
To: 'semea@doos.com'
Subject: more...

Semea –

On the sad history side, the Mushroom Master said he and his wife were teachers. Her father was deported to Siberia by the Russians, and suffered. He did return. I read a biography of a restoration expert who was deported, and when he returned a decade later, was not allowed into the university where he had been a medical student. He was able to learn architecture restoration as an apprentice and now is an expert with a reputation. Long story in a magazine about the deportations. Over 280,000 "threatening or suspect" people were deported. Conditions were: below freezing all the time, rustic dormitories, little food, people dying every day. It was slow torture and nearly sure death. A review of a book called A Stolen Youth says they were put on barges that slowly took them into the tundra of the Arctic Circle. Very little grew there. There were a few shacks. They were supposed to build a fish processing plant, which turned out to be a bunch of tables in the open air. It got dark most of the day and froze after August. People died of things like typhus every day.

Where the Germans came in and killed off more than 200,000 Jews fairly quickly (nearly all that were in Lithuania at the time), the Russians removed about the same number of a different segment of the population for a slow torture in slave labor. Some of those who survived were left with weakened health. I hear that our uncle's family were eligible for deportation (as our family would have been, had they stayed) due to his origins among the gentry, but a kind-hearted former employee of our grandfather, in charge of the deportation lists, kept striking their names off when they came up.

When the Germans kicked the Soviets out of Lithuania on June 22, 1941, it took three days to complete the occupation of the whole country. The locals found, in closets and safe, long lists of names of people whom the Soviets still wanted to deport had they had more time. People like our parents learned they were on those lists. That is why, when they knew the Soviets were coming back, they fled overnight.

Deportation was a familiar fate, by then, and they knew how it would happened based on real experience.

There are so many personal tragedies alive in current folks. There was speculation about who helped whom, and who didn't help, when the Devil came. Which side everyone took. How they managed to recover from near death, and returned to have children, to start schools, to restore art, and to make a life. I heard someone say you could not start a school before 1991, under the Soviets. And now you could.

Semea, think that you and I could have spent our lives processing fish in the tundra for decades...

I had a long conversation in a bar with a fellow American émigré. He said that mass killing of Jews, Poles, Prussians, etc., has a long tradition. Illegal emigration from Lithuania/Russia/Poland, and its underground "railways," has a long tradition. Ghettos have a long tradition as a community's way of retreating into a closed area in order to preserve their way of life. Mass deportations (to nearly sure death) and "death marches" seem to be a preferred Soviet method of controlling things. Special rules for special populations have a long tradition. The invaders force the education system to adopt the conquering country's language has been going on for centuries. That's why Lithuanians tend to know Polish and Russian very well.

The events of the 1940's through several decades were especially horrific and extreme. There are books just issued that argue: "Lithuanians *really helped* Jews escape and survive," "There *really was* armed resistance to Russians and Germans, by Lithuanians and Jews," "The genocide in Lithuania was *uniquely* aided by locals," "The Jews in the Ghetto *succeeded* in resisting, and in glorifying their culture against all odds."

When I was in Germany, every weekly edition of the Spiegel, it seemed, was processing "what actually happened" in WWII. In Lithuania, these topics were not allowed in public until 1991. They are just starting to process "what actually happened." This is fairly late in the lives of those who directly lived it and who can provide the facts. That in itself is painful. After a long public silence, they want the world to know: "look at the awful thing that happened to me thirty years ago."

I did find a few trinkets that I like. Some old Soviet military medals. Little books that look like the kind that were forbidden under the Soviets. They were printed outside the country and smuggled in.

I bought a small wooden carving of an angel. It is not your typical Christmas angel. This one shows the animist streak in Lithuanians. Lithuanians were the last to adopt Christianity in Europe. I think they did it to survive. It is like voodoo in Haiti. They took on the symbols of Christianity but kept some of the native beliefs. From the outside they look like Christians but there are strange twists and symbols added on, and a lot of magic. This angel has a white, mournful face. See the picture I've attached. It also has a slot in the back, where you can insert a message to "animate" it for a personal reason.

I rented a bike and toured Uzupe (Across the River). I had the impression that this part of town is the "underbelly" of Vilnius. It is small. I can walk there, and several miles within it. The old town is the pride and joy. The old town is also site of recent horror, the Vilna Ghetto. Uzupe is Greenwich Village, with workers, artisans, and artists, living cheap. Might have been outside the original medieval castle. What is surprising is how much in the city is the same across seven centuries. How could each patch of a few square miles stay the same for so long? Is it that stone makes it harder to tear things down and rebuild? The stone basically "owns" parts of town. I don't understand why the entire old city is only on one side of the river. There is so much open land on the other side.

The Soviets built their housing to the north, creating ugly suburbs of concrete high rises. I wonder if Russians aren't missing a "gene for aesthetics." Soviets just did not like much color. Think of the color in Asian Indian fabrics, Maharajah palaces, Guatemalan cloth, Malaysian batik, and Asian wood temples. Did Russians grow up in an Artic wasteland and therefore they could not imagine color, texture, and design? Even concrete can be poured into forms, like Southwestern adobe, that is something more than square and grey. Few trees. No softness, no coddling of the eye. That's it: no coddling. They do have some palaces from the royal times of old. The Soviets are proud of having soul, but that soul is nothing like the Latin soul, like Gabriel Marquez' fantasies of ghosts, magic, passion, dance, anguish. It has the color of Arctic night. The communists did not seem to celebrate human creativity

24

or pleasure or individuality. I wonder if profound communists ever sit back and think, "Wow, I wouldn't mind going to Mardi Gras for a change of scene."

Time to go to bed. – Zenius

Attachment: sadangelface1.jpg

Attachment: sadangelface2.jpg

Attachment: mardigras.jpg

Mingen, Zenius [zen@ulink.net]
Sent: August 24, 2003
To: 'semea@doos.com'
Subject: why medieval beds are high

Semea –

One of my favorite colleagues is a young woman who studied in Bulgaria for 7 years, from early 90's to late. I asked how she could afford to do that. It was Soros Foundation funds. She got a Ph.D. She studied there in English. Married a Serbian who now teaches history & political science at Vilnius University, in English. Her sister, who married an American and lives in America, is thinking of sending her children back to Vilnius University because it is cheap. Not comparable quality, but still. By the way, as many people as have a relative who was deported to hell by the Russians seem to have a relative who emigrated to the U.S., like us.

We visited the Lithuanian Science Council and the Academy of Sciences with a small informal tour. The building entry is a large, carved, wooden door, about 4 feet by 20 feet. You need both hands to pull it open. Feels like Harry Potter or Alice in Wonderland. Inside, there were passages where you had to duck for the low ceilings. (Were people 4' tall in the middle ages?) All of these ancient doors do not close tightly, and the ceilings are waaaay up there, so I imagine when the bitter Nordic winter sets in ("10 months of the year"), it probably feels like the middle ages. However, people had very nice offices inside, with couches and coat closets, and chocolates for guests. And Ikea-type furniture.

Later I learned that the low passage-ways are intended to keep the heated air from escaping the high-ceiling rooms. That means that the lowest four feet of air is generally cooler, and moving. Maybe that explains high medieval beds.

One of the scientists quickly got to the question: "Are you basically recruiting Lithuanian scientists to leave?" After I assured him, he asked very directly who my parents were. This is like asking what is your caste in India. I was tempted to make things up. He wanted to know the details of their emigration. I said they worked very hard, in America, for many years. That turns out to be an issue for the people left behind. They imagine that Lithuanians go to the U.S. and "do the hard jobs." What they don't realize is that immigrants get past those "hard jobs" very quickly. You scrub floors and take courses like our parents did, and about a decade later you are better off. Better off than someone who stayed behind and scrubbed floors in Lithuania.

I am reading a book about emigration from Lithuania. In the early 1900's there were over 800,000 Lithuanians in the U.S. There are about that many now. In the U.S. they had their own newspapers (300!), churches, language schools, unions in America. They even brought with them a nationalist movement to separate their identity from the immigrant Poles. They had a campaign to get the U.S. census to identify them separately. Strikingly, the exile community has typically been very insular, mostly Catholic, and nationalistic. Many did not learn English very well. The émigrés seem very much indeed like the orthodox Jews in Lithuania, who tried to maintain as much isolation from others as possible, to preserve language, culture and religion – resisting assimilation! Apparently this base of émigrés in the U.S. has been a great asset for business investment here. In fact, a number of locals are recruiting me as "one of our own," appealing to me to give back to the motherland.

A lot of emigration through the whole century was a secret escape. In the 1900s, a Russian edict said it was forbidden to encourage people to leave. Emigration was considered treason. Most of the emigrants were illiterate (except for Jews). Most of them had someone in the family who had "gone ahead" already – as in our family.

On a lark, I put a slip of paper in my wooden angel. It says "you are that" in Sanskrit – "tat tvam asi" which in Lithuanian is "tu esi tas." You probably know this Buddhist principle. "We are god, and god is us, and all reality is us, and we are part of continual creation." So my little wooden angel is now the bearer of the Ultimate Message. I never liked the Christian "God is love," where god is an external agent, like a parent, who watches over you and protects you and judges you. This angel really seems a Buddhist: the sad face, the focus on suffering in face of karmic challenges, one lifetime at a time.

Zenius

From: Mingen, Semea [semea@doos.com]
Sent: August 27, 2003
To: 'zen@ulink.net'
Subject: Re: why medieval beds are high

Zen –

Did you know that moss can survive a long spell of dryness by ceasing photosynthesis? It becomes dormant, and reawakens only when rain falls again. Do you think souls of humans do that when the light of goodness goes out? To stop trying to grow, shut down defensively, and wait out a black period? I hope so.

I have read that hypnosis induces the same physiological state and mental brain waves of meditation, and shock. For example, if you bounce a chicken on its legs a few times, it goes into a catatonic state. Which is of course a natural protection – block all inputs, concentrate blood in vital organs (which the brain is not). Wait for the threat to pass. We can of course hypnotize ourselves, or enter ourselves into a meditative state. I wonder if prisoners of war have do this? That is, enter a personal transcendence zone. Go back to a prior, more pleasant life? Turn off caring, and anger. They say the victims of extreme violence actually lose consciousness at a certain threshold, so they are "not there" after a certain point. It is only the observers who have to face intolerable truths about man's capacity to inflict pain on others. The victims have built-in shields of unconsciousness.

Still awake and green here – Semea

From: Mingen, Zenius [zen@ulink.net]
Sent: August 31, 2003
To: 'semea@doos.com'
Subject: creepy stuff

Semea -

I returned from a long day at the lab, having had to work through some broken equipment and make sure our samples were o.k. There were a lot of tensions while Malke and Dalia went through a period of feeling that the break was due to negligence on Pijus' part. It turned out to be innocent, and independent of anybody's actions – just the wear and tear of a part that we had barely noticed before.

When I got home, however, already a little discombobulated from the disruptions at work, I found that my books had been shifted around in the apartment. I do not have a maid, and no visitors, really. My copy of "Three Seductive Ideas" has been on the bedroom chest of drawers since I arrived, and "Parasites of the Tropics" was in the living room on a side table, where I had been reading it. I found "Three Seductive Ideas" on the kitchen counter, and "Parasites" was on the bathroom floor. As if someone had picked them up to browse, and then got distracted and set them down. This was most disturbing because it was a sign that someone had been inside the apartment. I am really upset, but I don't know who to check with – who would have a key except the landlord who lives out of town? A landlord does not go around reading your books! A landlord checks the appliances, and light switches, and dirt in the kitchen, maybe.

My valuables are mostly electronic. I think I will start hiding them when I am out.

I am too distracted to write more now. I was tempted to call you but it was 5 a.m. for you, and maybe there is an innocent explanation I am too flustered to find right now.
Z.

From: Mingen, Zenius [zen@ulink.net]
Sent: September 8, 2003
To: 'semea@doos.com'
Subject: beet soup

Semea –

We had a visitor to the lab today from Hungary. He has written a book about the lives of his parents, who survived the Hungarian uprising.

It has been a week since the "book relocation" mystery. Things calmed down pretty well. I went to a cello concert at the Philharmonic, for

$7. Apparently there is one row of seats in the orchestra – the row which is facing the wide aisle in the middle, giving it maximum leg room and visibility – that is reserved for important guests. My ticket was for a seat in the balcony, but there were not very many people there, and the ushers wanted me to go below so they could close the balcony. Well, I took a nice seat in the middle of the middle row of the orchestra, which was completely empty. An usher immediately came up to me and said "you may not sit here." I asked why, and she said I had to take a seat in any other row. I replied that they had just bumped me from the balcony and asked me to sit anywhere down below. She was very jumpy. When a group of people approached "my" middle row, she came back, and said "Please, please, sir, move." Someone behind this row advised that it was customary to seat dignitaries here. He pointed out one of the ministers in the government. That's how I discovered these were informal "box seats." Still cannot figure out why the usher would not outright say it. Maybe an old communist taboo on admitting that some people are more equal than others.

The Latvians are about to vote whether to join the European Union. One of their leaders says the goal of Latvia is "to be another boring West European country." He is not worried about being invaded by immigrants: "We don't have the kind of economy, the opportunities or even the climate that would attract massive amounts of immigrants." Count on that Nordic climate! Another fear is that the young people will all emigrate (escaping that rough climate and limited opportunities...). The EU is the place to be. I heard an American say that his daughter was born in Austria, and he was going to get her citizenship rights in the EU, because that would give her access to EU's universities and jobs. The EU is about the size of the U.S. The U.S. is no longer the place to be!

OK, food adventures: Ukranian cold beet and mushroom salad; pot of cheese and mushrooms; crepes with apples and sweet sour cream. (Crepes with anything are great.)

I bought a bouquet of flowers for a birthday in the lab. The shop girl used one hand as the "vase" and arranged the flowers in it, adding three different kinds of greens (free), and tying the whole thing tight with straw, which she cut artistically. Then, she cut the bottoms even. Like a tea ceremony.

Apparently Italians are the biggest adopters of Lithuanian orphans. They like large families and will take a batch of older children. The Danes are also high on the list. Americans are lower because they only want infants, and those are scarce.

I did not write last week because my computer got a virus. I don't use the computer at home to dial out much, and don't bring any files home, so I have no idea how this happened. It would freeze for about ten minutes, and show a lot of activity on the hard drive (I could hear it grinding away). It was really scary – I had no idea what it was doing, I was locked out, and it could have been scrambling the whole system! Then 10 minutes later, all normal. Then after about 10 minutes, again, it was taken over. I could not find anything suspicious, but then, how often does anybody look at every directory, and even recognize any "alien" files? I took the laptop to a shop, and they ran a virus check, and could not find anything! That is even worse. I paid only about $30 for the virus check, but still, have a creepy feeling of vulnerability – something is lurking that I don't know, and cannot stamp out.

I guess you can control garden pests better than this!
Cheers, Z.

From: Mingen, Zenius [zen@ulink.net]
Sent: September 20, 2003
To: 'semea@doos.com'
Subject: languages

Semea –

Basketball is as big as football in U.S. or soccer in Europe. The Lit's won over Sweden and then played the Spanish for world finals. When they won, I was at a street fair, and guys were leaning out of windows screaming "We won! We won!" About a half hour later they emptied the bars and appeared in cars and groups, driving, honking, shouting, for the next few hours. Completely blocking those narrow, cobble-stone streets. Wearing a Lithuanian flag. High-fiving strangers.

The next night, they won the finals over Spain, and I was wakened by honking throughout the city after midnight.

They really like noisy car gizmos and phone sounds. There is an advertisement to the hip young people to call up a certain number, and identify their type of phone, and download (for a fee) a "signature" display logo, or cartoon, and a melody. Can choose from among 40 popular songs. (When I was in Germany years ago, people really hated "techno-pop" and would rebuke offenders in public.)

I joined a tour of a local business innovation center with visitors from various countries in Eastern Europe. It was a motley group – you can no longer tell nationalities from faces because there has been so much mixing in this part of the world. National boundaries have shifted 4 or 5 times during the 20th century – something most Americans could not imagine. That means your children could start school in one language and then have to learn two or more others to finish, and maybe end up having to take exams in yet another. People seem to be comfortable with the polyglot flow. When a staff member starts describing something in Polish, the visitors responded in Polish. A vendor on the street starts with Russian, and gets a response in Russian. No pretension, as in, "I am speaking to this strange lower-ranked person in my society," just, "Hello, what's up." The dominant language has not always been dominant. I think there is some sympathy with the difficulty of forcing everyone into one language, so the people who can do it switch for the comfort of the person they are talking to. It is like multiple linguistic realities coinciding – at any moment, the strata of Russian speakers connect while non-Russian speakers feel left out. Then the switch is pulled, and the Polish-savvy have the floor. You are left wondering what the heck they are talking about, in this exchange of sounds.

I cannot imagine all these languages are emotionally neutral to the speakers, however. There is some intellectual satisfaction in being able to join in on various channels, but I think we all have loaded every language with associations that are covert. When I first got here, I was just amazed to be in a Lithuanian-speaking world. We spoke Lithuanian only at home, and it was our language of intimacy. When we were in public and had to confer privately, we switched to Lithuanian, pretty sure that no one (like the shoe salesman) could "tune in" to our secret language. It was my language of trust, and privacy. To hear the bus driver speak to me, or the book store clerk – it was a shock. My immediate reaction was trust and familiarity. I had to remember that the Mafia here also speaks Lithuanian. I guess it doesn't hurt to feel kinder toward Lithuanian speakers who are total strangers. A powerful thing. I guess I would have to hear a lot of bad people saying nasty things to erase the association. Watch some violent TV in Lithuanian.

Although I love German, I am painfully aware of it as the language of Nazis. We've seen enough movies of cruelty, barking military orders, screams in German, to tense up at the sound. Goethe must be having a fit in heaven.

Zen

From:	Mingen, Semea [semea@doos.com]
Sent:	September 24, 2003
To:	'zen@ulink.net'
Subject:	Re: languages

Zenius –

Speaking of language. I went to walk a maze the other day. It is designed just like the maze in the Cathedral at Chartres created in 1235 AD. Three of us went. You walk in complete silence of course – the point is meditation, not chatter and bonding. I was curious about the combination of walking and movement with contemplation. We started out at different times so as to avoid collisions. The space is very small, actually. People are walking in tight circles around each other in the space of a large room.

At my second or third turn, I got a clear image of Dad. He was showing me, on the banks of Baker Lake, how to clean a fish. He was smiling, and obviously enjoying the slithery weight of the big salmon in his palm, and waving his gut knife in the air as he explained. I saw the guts slide out and hit the water in the lake, and then fish roe shoved out with his thumb. He was smiling, in the sun, and purely satisfied with his catch and with me there with him. I tried to ask mentally "What are you really trying to show me?" but stopped myself. I think gutting the fish was the whole point. However, even more important, was the feeling of him, sweaty in the sun, smelling the water and the fish, and hunkered down together, balancing in a squat over the lapping water.

I asked Adrian how you were doing, and he said you would be turning to me soon. I know you don't believe in psychics so take it for nothing. I like having a leg in a possible future. –S.

Attachment: chartresmaze.jpg

From: Mingen, Zenius [zen@ulink.net]
Sent: September 28, 2003
To: 'semea@doos.com'
Subject: icons

Semea –

I think Dad was telling you to go fishing and quit walking in circles. Have some real fun!

Vladimir was telling me that paganism has never really gone away here. There are beliefs in sacred spaces – fields, waters, groves, and symbols, and meanings attributed to natural forces. The adoption of Christianity was forced. There were unrelenting attacks from Crusaders in the 13ᵗʰ Century. Conversion was a way to buy off aggression. For a long time, Christianity only really took hold in the few cities. The Jesuits sent missionaries into the villages, destroyed the wooden relics, and basically desecrated the traditional holy places of pagans. How's that for winning souls?

I remember that the Muslims invading India cut off the noses of Hindu gods, as their idea of a religious "rape."

A lot of the symbols here seem Celtic to me. It is interesting that, as with voodoo in Haiti, the natives preserved their symbols by dressing them in Catholic images. Almost as if to say, "Let's be nice to these invaders and pretend to like their icons." More likely, it was "They'll kill us if we don't pretend to like their icons, let's pretend to convert!" The Catholic "authorities" were satisfied, and did not work as hard to differentiate and destroy the native icons. Each side feeling the other is blind to the truth. There are people who lump Catholics and communists together, in their methods of using fear and righteousness to combat disagreement. As usual, religion and politics are completely mixed. Vladimir says there are thousands of pagans reviving their movement. That seems a lot, in a country of 3.5 million. I think they have cohorts in the other Baltic countries, and maybe internationally now, with the help of the internet. I wonder if there is a cohesive international movement – that shares pagan beliefs regardless of their country and its local politics. Do many pagans identify with each other? (Like atheists seem to ...)

There is both shame and pride in the fact that Lithuania "was the last European country to accept Christianity." The Christians point out this fact with disdain, and the pagan-believers note it with pride. One web site had a plea from an anxious reader: "Why are you doing this [reviving paganism]? Why are you proud to call yourself pagan?" i.e. "What is wrong with you? You are making us look bad."

One of the seasonal celebrations is a Day of the Dead. Do you know the origins of that? Do you know if they are celebrating the same Dead as the Mexicans, and the same ways? Zenius

From: Mingen, Semea [semea@doos.com]
Sent: October 1, 2003
To: 'zen@ulink.net'
Subject: Re: icons

Z –

As you know, a lot of people talk to the dead, not just Mexicans and Lit pagans. Madame Blavatsky and the Theosophists built up a whole international spiritualist movement in Victorian times. They held séances. Tied in with ghosts too – the attempt on the part of the dead to appear and converse with the living. Seances were quite the fashion in Victorian times.

Did you know about her book *The Secret Doctrine*? It was dictated to her by the "Masters," who were, of course, spirits. Master Morya and Master Koot Hoomi. To confirm the validity of her claim, the Master M. himself left a "certificate" written in red crayon, vouching that the Doctrine was dictated by him. The "occult truths" he dictated were the esoterica/mysteries rooted in the Indian Brahmanic doctrines, alleged to be the "original knowledge of the Manasaputras." A contemporary (and living) Brahman in India who started to help her with some corrections to the Doctrine stopped, because the teachings were supposed to be kept secret. He distrusted Westerners, and, he could not accept the fact that the teachings were coming from one of his own spirit Masters through a *woman*. Spiritualists eagerly waited over four years while Blavatsky produced it, and then sections of it were stolen or lost in the logistics of sending copies to India and back from England, getting it to printers, etc. That must have been an exciting time – 1880's – with all the British discovering India's classics.

All I know about the Mexican Day of the Dead: November 2nd, families clean up grave sites and decorate them with marigolds and favorite things to entice the dead to return for a visit. Everybody parties. The kids are a little spooked. It is remembrance and celebration, communion, and perspective on life and death. The crafts are just great – a mockery of death by depicting a dead choir or a dead doctor. Many little figures about 3 inches tall. Dead people cooking dinner or selling vegetables. Dead lovers, especially. They get to relive favorite earthly moments. Maybe all the fun makes death less scary.

Speaking of disdain. In spite of reading so much about religions, you still seem to hold them all at arm's length. Tell me, what do you think happens when you die? Should we just pay somebody to stuff you in a garbage bag and haul you away to the nearest incinerator for sanitary disposal, according to scientific definitions of "sanitary?" I think your scientific interest and passion (yes, passion) for debunking all beliefs and sentiments about eternity and spirit is just an elaborate scheme you must keep constructing. Don't you see that that scheme is like a huge piece of embroidery that you cannot stop working on? Can't an anti-spirit belief system itself turn into a closed belief system? It is externally determined – every squiggly fact you find about "irrational" or "unscientific" belief further determines your dogma. Anti- anything is something, and it is dependent, and wedded to its root inspiration. Zenius, drop the conceptual facades and even the words, and feel your soul.

Those zealous synapses you cultivate in your head are quite a diversion.

With love, Semea

Attachment: dayofdead.jpg

From: Mingen, Zenius [zen@ulink.net]
Sent: October 12, 2003
To: 'semea@doos.com'
Subject: survivors

Semea –

I read an account of a survivor of the German Sutthof camp. This was Balys Sruoga, who was born in 1986. He was about 47 years old in 1943 when the Germans decided he was a threat, and rounded him up with a bunch of other intellectuals to keep him from leading possible resistance movements. He seems to have been an apolitical professor of literature, well established and known, in a small country with few universities. Published a lot. He kept notes during the encampment, somehow, and when he finally got free of German and Russian incarcerations, he wrote his story of more than 300 pages from a lot of notes. He died soon after, his health broken.

He says the Germans really liked camps, of all kinds. They were good at organizing temporary structures, managing bunches of people, and taking care of all the administrative logistics of camps. What a handy talent in war time, huh?   Lots of trained people. Probably had seminars for camp administrators – how to deal with food, elimination, discipline, and then, of course, the protocols for torturing prisoners.

The occupying Germans were angry that Lithuanians would not freely enlist and join their forces to fight the Russians. The officers were being held accountable for enlistment quotas back in the mother country, so they had to think of incentives to recruit Lithuanian soldiers. They used intimidation. They rounded people up, early or late in the day, when they were home. Mom described people staying away from all night, to avoid being home for raids. They went after a few university professors so the students would get the message.

The details of Stuffhof are horrific, of course. There is progressive and rapid humiliation, as belongings are taken away, soldiers beat everyone whimsically, and then they inflict the depravations of cold, hunger, sleeplessness right away. We are so fragile! Yet Sruoga survived such things as, in year two or three of the ordeal, being marched out to forests to lift trees while suffering diarrhea, cold, weakness. His story says that we are not fragile at all. Many prisoners died every day, but many more were killed for small rebellious acts or unlucky incidents. They would be alive except that some joe-nazi with a sadistic or just angry personality needed a new victim that day.

The hardest part reading these accounts is that humans are torturing other humans. Once in a while there is a civil, respectful exchange – a comment acknowledging humanity, like "why don't you sleep over here away from the other prisoners sick with typhus?" And then, wham, over the head, possibly fatal.

The irony of Sruoga's liberation is that, after the German imprisonment, he was subjected to torture by the Russians who tried to establish his loyalty to communism. He died only a few years after the Soviets took over Lithuania. His manuscript in Lithuanian was suppressed but finally appeared in 1957, ten years after his death. He had managed to have at least one child, however, and his granddaughter, who had never met him and grew up in the U.S., translated the book into English.

These personal stories also give new meaning to "mid career derailment." Imagine management seminars in the U.S. training people in their 30's and 40's to succeed and advance in organizations, and how to look for signs of adversity or lack of support as they enter leadership positions, and to reevaluate themselves and their organizations, and to look for ways to improve their "fit" with others. Wham, over the head. No food, clothing, sleep, and lots of pain and disease. I guess it is suffering at different levels of Maslow's pyramid. Is it less palpable to be actually hit in the head or "thwarted in self actualization?" Of course, when natural disasters hit us, they hit our basic needs. An earthquake can make people afraid to go in their houses, as they mourn the death of family members, and are left with no clean water, no food, the middle of winter, too cold to sleep. Maslow talks about our hierarchy of needs from basic to abstract. I wonder whether you feel different if you feel that the agent of your distress is impersonal (nature), or if you think it is human malice and politics. I would find the hardest pill to swallow would be blatant human malice – a stupid man with a gun who wants to hurt you because you are one of "your kind," and he is grouchy.

Hope your sun is shining – Z.

From: Mingen, Semea [semea@doos.com]
Sent: October 25, 2003
To: 'zen@ulink.net'
Subject: Re: survivors

Zenius –

Some of your letters make me want to play with kittens.

I can't help wishing you were working in Florence and Tuscany, and telling me about unimaginable feats of artistic achievement in Italy. Culinary delights, happy street musicians, the glory of centuries of art. I know you are going to say some of the people who "contributed" to the creation of art did not exactly volunteer for the job, and got their only reward in fatigue and the allowance to live another day…

Maybe I should put you on a beach in the South Seas, where food is plentiful, the natives unexploited and unthreatened for centuries, getting up each day to take a walk with the warm surf splashing their toes. Making pretty leis and fabrics, and taking all day to cook delicious subtle meals, except for the luscious afternoon nap in the shade, with the breeze keeping bugs away. Plump naked babies running around in the sand, like cherubs.

How many people in the world use their wealth to insulate them from personal discomfort, and distance themselves from awareness of the discomfort of others? They do need servants. I wonder if there is such a thing as a happy servant who feels adequately compensated and o.k. with the inequities inherent in working to help others stay clear of unpleasantness and discomfort.

'Xcuse, I have to find a kitten. Play a little Bach while we frolic.

Semea

From: Mingen, Zenius [zen@ulink.net]
Sent: November 2, 2003
To: 'semea@doos.com'
Subject: crow

Semea –

A crow crashed into my window this morning. It is Sunday and I was reading in a chair near the window. I was startled, and rushed up to

41

see if it was still alive. Not only was it alive, it started hammering the glass! I was afraid to pull up the window because it looked so aggressive. Bang bang bang, swipe the beak on the sill for a minute, then bang bang bang. I thought, what a crazy, clumsy crow! They are supposed to be really smart. I've seen them steal bags of popcorn in Calcutta, and then fly to a communal roof, open the bag, and share it. BANG BANG BANG. I was afraid the window would break. I rushed to the fridge and cut a piece of cheese, and then opened the window a crack and slipped it out. While I pulled the window up, it seemed to check out my torso against the glass, as if to think, o.k. where should I peck first? As I slipped the cheese out, it cawed angrily and loudly. Have you ever been inches away from a screaming crow? I jumped back. That seems to be what it wanted, and it slipped a piece of paper over the sill. Then it screamed again, just for good measure, keeping me away. Took up the cheese and jumped off into nowhere.

The paper was a drawing in red crayon, rather elaborate:

Semea, what do you make of this?   -Z

Attachment: redcrayon.jpg

From: Mingen, Semea [semea@doos.com]
Sent: November 3, 2003
To: 'zen@ulink.net'
Subject: Re: crow

Zenius –
Kittens. I told you to play with KITTENS, not angry scary crows! I want to know what YOU make of it?

By the way, my ethnographer says that the ancient or pagan Lit's also celebrate a Day of the Dead. Depending on where you are in the country (how did all those tiny areas maintain separate beliefs??) the souls of the dead come back on November 1st. Some think to the cemetery, some think to the home. At home, folks will prepare a meal and share food with the dead souls. Candles can be involved, to show them the way. The family might make little rolls for each soul to be welcomed, and then give the rolls to beggars who are obliged to pray for them. Like spiritualists, they think the dead are still among us, in another form. (When the Christians came along, this was associated with Purgatory.) So this day, called Ilges for longing, is a day of getting together, just once a year. Is it the longing of the dead for life, or the longing of the living for the dead?

My friend says there were also old Lithuanian beliefs that you should burn, and not bury, the dead, and that there are other practices that echo those in Indian Vedic tradition. No surprise, since they both originated from Indo-European tribes.
Semea

From: Mingen, Zenius [zen@ulink.net]
Sent: November 8, 2003
To: 'semea@doos.com'
Subject: storks

Semea –
When driving in the countryside in the north, I saw stork's nests for the first time. These are about 4 foot diameter and 1-2 foot deep nests, high up on top of a pole. In fact, they rest right on top of the tip of poles about 30 feet tall. This picture completely threw me. I immediately

thought: do storks have a "gene for engineering?" School children could have a module to study: how a stork starts a nest on the tip of pole, and builds it out to this huge symmetrical structure of branches and leaves into a cushion the size of a bean bag chair. I kept this excitement to myself. Two days later I bothered to ask: how DO the storks do that? The answer was: the farmers mount a wheel on top end of the pole, like a platform, to invite the storks to nest. Oh.

There was a jazz festival on the weekend. Very exotic stuff: groups combining Middle Eastern and Japanese styles. Evoking folk roots from darkest wherever – Russia, Latvia, Mongolia. I bought an expensive ticket to the Russian theater, an old battered structure. $7 got me seat in the orchestra of a small theater with two tiers of balcony. The wooden seats felt like they were taken from a bus station where you want to discourage loiterers – the 90 degree severe angle of the back actually leaning forward, pitching you forward. The first group was o.k. – a magnificent Japanese saxophonist, playing with a mad drummer. The mad drummer was a skinny rumpled guy with long grey hair and an artificial leg that was too short. He was clearly a drumming genius, replicating Japanese Noh theater sounds and such. This was much like being in the garage with the musicians. The second group from Lithuania were known for having invented "noise jazz." This consisted of taking advantage of the screeching sound you get from electric guitars, and waving, intensely, some very fine long hair cut in a large bowl cut. I thought his neck was going to snap, for the sensitivity he seemed to have for screeching sounds, snapping his hair forward and back and side to side. Then another guy started making creative nonsense noises into a microphone. Feeling overwhelmed by my sensitivity to "noise jazz," I had to leave.

Siemens, a German company, held an Oktoberfest party for their employees next door to the laboratory. In the middle of a huge inner courtyard of the 13th century church, workmen constructed a semi-dome, using something like a giant erector set. (Yes, that dates me pre-Legos.) Then they covered it with a bright yellow canvas. This was about 100 feet by 300 feet area, 50 feet high, caterpillar shape. We did hear some live music rehearsals – Italian love songs. The event must have occurred for just one night. The set-up which had taken a week took another week to

44

tear down. (How's that for employment for the locals?) All of the materials and maybe 500 guests had to enter the courtyard through one 13ᵗʰ century stone archway just high & wide enough for one car. Not bad for a fall company party! I wonder if the monks used it as party space too.

Speaking of cheap labor. We were talking about the unemployment rate, and how, everywhere, it disguises the number of people who have given up seeking work, and, those who won't take the jobs that are available. Pre 1990, under the Soviets, all the college graduates, and everyone else, were assigned a job. For example, a librarian might be given a job in a small farm village in the north, where they would tend to library books, haul the wood for the stove, keep a cow for food, repair the building, and such. Now, a library school graduate may *decline* to take that kind of job, and be unemployed. So under the new free market system, they are unemployed, but under the communists they would have been employed (albeit unhappily).

Zenius

From: Mingen, Zenius [zen@ulink.net]
Sent: November 16, 2003
To: 'semea@doos.com'
Subject: old trees

Semea –

We just had a visiting committee talk about global trends in HIV/AIDS. Three million people are dying each year, while 5 million are newly infected. The number living with AIDS is up to 40 million. These numbers are incomprehensible. More than half of all of this is concentrated in sub-saharan Africa. More than 2 million people died there last year, while in North American it is about 15,000. That means a difference in magnitude, between our continents, of more than 100 times.

I cannot stop thinking about what this says about humanity. We've seen enough world-wide to know that the epidemic starts with injecting-drug users and male homosexuals – small, marginalized groups.

Then it spreads quickly to heterosexuals. In Africa, the trend has reached the point where young women are 2.5 times more likely to get infected than young men. There are two countries in which 40% of the population is infected. Children are getting infected through their young mothers.

In fact, the estimates of HIV prevalence are being calculated from the prevalence of infection among *pregnant women*. What a horrible index! That estimate is only possible if the pregnant women in that country are ever tested or gain access to any medical attention. If they don't test them, then the stats look good. Undercounting is a great excuse for denying there is a problem.

I fear for our future! Whole countries are going to disappear as the adults die, leaving children who can barely grow up alone before they join the ranks of the dying. Who's going to produce food, and maintain a society – workforce, police, shops, schools? I've heard that university faculties have a lot of vacancies – lots of opportunity for the young – because of rapid attrition due to infection and death. Who is teaching the young to prepare them for the positions or jobs? We talk about the transfer of "institutional knowledge" in our workplaces, and primitive societies worry about the transmission of traditional knowledge. What if the life space contracts back to where it was twenty centuries ago – where few people live to 40?

I feel foolish working on such a tiny piece of the problem – how to design more drugs to keep up with the development of drug-resistant strains of the virus. We should be hysterical, by now, about prevention. We are not even hysterical about managing the impacts – millions of orphans, no counseling, no testing, and no intervention to prevent mother-to-child transmission. At least we should stop the infection of children!! This thing crosses societies and cultures, and we all, ALL, don't want to deal with the fact that this is mass suicide through unprotected sex. Is there no one society that is open enough to say: let's educate, thoroughly, every man, woman, and child, every day, to avoid infection and transmission.

When I was in India even a decade ago it seemed to me people – who were at the time 95% illiterate – had mostly not grasped the concept of germs and bacteria. Whole villages bathed in one stagnant pond, in which they also washed their animals, rinsed their dishes, and maybe even defecated. They defecated everywhere, especially in rice paddies to fertilize the crops, moving a wooden platform around the paddy to spread the fertilizer. Many had worms, chronically. In the cities, the street vendors simply rinsed a tea cup in a bucket of brown water for the next customer. Because they believed that water, by itself, is purifying. They had not grasped that there are invisible things IN the water that infect humans. Well, with some education, and lots of coaching, people "got" that you had to boil drinking water, and water could be "polluted" and was unclean. But then often the ice was not made from boiled water. Why boil water if you are going to make ice?

Same thing with HIV. Ignorance about where it sits, and how it gets to you. And because it is stigmatized – associated with deviant social groups, and with "dirty sex" – people won't talk about it, admit infection, get tested, or ask sexual partners to use protection. How much longer can we all pretend before we are surrounded by sick and dying neighbors? Should we send tours to Africa to make the point? We spend so much on good teeth, nice hair, low cholesterol, and argue about spending tax dollars for music classes, or new roads, or museums. All that is going to be MOOT. Just because we (globally) have to have sex, and we want to stay stupid about it.

Sorry, Semea. I am feeling isolated, and overwhelmed. As if this lab work is just another project. I might as well be studying how trees age. Z.

From: Mingen, Semea [semea@doos.com]
Sent: November 21, 2003
To: 'zen@ulink.net'
Subject: Re: old trees

Zenius –

You must resist the conceit that you will save humanity with your science project. It will destroy your spirit, because it is an impossible goal. As long as you do something every day that contributes to the solution, you are on "the right path."

Humanity has survived some pretty awful major disasters. The plague, for one. Maybe these are population "corrections," and they are more shocking because the numbers keep getting larger. Did they ever figure out why the dinosaurs disappeared? Was it stupidity?

Can you find turkey there? –S.

From: Mingen, Zenius [zen@ulink.net]
Sent: November 30, 2003
To: 'semea@doos.com'
Subject: corrections

Semea –

I guess I am more used to population "corrections" – like stock market "corrections" – made by people intentionally, as in killing off the group you don't want.

Just like computer models of stock markets, we have a computer model for HIV infection, developed for Asia. There are experts that predict more infected people in Asia by 2010 than in Africa now. For example, a 4% rate in India means 25 million people. The Asian Epidemic Model takes real facts unique to an Asian country, and predicts the future. For example, if .4% of women are sex workers, and they average one client a day, and do not use condoms 75% of the time, and their clients include 10% of adult males. Or, if drug users are .5% of males, and they share needles two-thirds of the time, and inject 2.5 times per day, what is the effect on infection rates? It is showing that if you stop the drug user infections, you slow the epidemic if not stop it. But if you don't, and the number of female sex workers and clients doubles, you could get to infection rates of 23% of men and 9% of women. We are able to trace the path of types of viruses along actual heroin trafficking roads. In the 1990's, 20% of men in Cambodia and Thailand hired sex workers. Women, fortunately, are still fairly monogamous, but that is changing with modernization. There are furious arguments about whose numbers or model are right. Unlike the stock market, this is not about fluctuations in wealth.

With AIDS, nobody is killing you off. Your society, however, chooses how vigorously to educate people in sex and especially sex as an act of infection, so that you will protect yourself vigorously. I agree that drug-injecting types are already self-destructive, so they are harder to convince that sharing needles is deadly. Could we get them to adopt safe ways of getting high? Is the fear of <u>deadly</u> infection enough motivation for them? I don't know. But the rest of us want to live to have sex again, not to mention raise children, and party, and go on vacation instead of wasting away. We've gotten children to wash their hands, and brush their teeth. Most people practice methods of personal hygiene that take time and are inconvenient, like flossing your teeth. Surely they could be persuaded that this thing you do (usually) with another person called sex needs to be done differently, with some inconvenience, for the sake of the quality and length of your life.

Well, I have to go floss my teeth. That other stuff is a non-issue for me now.

Zenius

From: Mingen, Zenius [zen@ulink.net]
Sent: December 10, 2003
To: 'semea@doos.com'
Subject: mad cat

Semea –

I was walking through narrow passages behind the main streets in the old town, where debris from renovation is piled up, and really old wood beams are still holding up thatched roofs, while the front façade is beautiful polished stone and new windows, looking like it might have in the 14ᵗʰ century. It is always shocking to see how workers will gut an old structure in the middle of town and be forced to hide the mess. How can you be discreet about trucks full of detritus? Back in this "alley" which was really like a series of tunnels between tiny courtyards, there were actually wooden "apartments" over a garage, also looking ancient and worn, and possibly places to live for people who don't live "in front." I don't know who lives in these places, or why, and am reminded I am really a stranger to the back rooms of Vilnius.

There was an old wooden barrel – the kind that we've seen used to catch rain water. A cat came leaping almost straight out of the fairly-deep barrel and raced up to me, howling. Usually a hungry cat will chase up after you and howl for food, so that's what I expected. But this cat tore ahead of me by ten feet, then flipped on its side, stretched to what seemed like four feet in length, blocking my way. It was black with specs of yellow – mongrel looking – but huge, and muscular. The yellow eyes glared at me between two paws reaching over its head, as if daring me to pass. I was stopped and didn't reach down, in case it was hostile. The behavior wasn't clear, for a cat. A cat trying to scare you would arch its back and raise its hair, and hiss. A cat begging for food would try to rub against your leg. This one was taking a good stretch at my expense, and seemingly intentionally. It was huge, like a small panther, and its size alone was startling. I could not imagine a feral cat getting so big. And being so outrageously bold with a human, baring its belly that way. I said "hey, cat" to break the tension for myself. The cat simply glared, and stretched again. I did not want to get within reach of its claws, so I moved slowly around it to the right, staying a few feet from the twitching tail. I swear, as I passed, it said "Boo." Human like. Honest. Like a person would say it to himself, to hear the sound. Semea, is that possible? Can a cat say a word like that?

It is amazing to imagine the different generations that have shared the glory of these old structures, inside and out. They have actually walked on the same floor, sat by the same window, cooked in the same kitchen, slept in the same space upstairs. In 1916, the census of Vilnius says the city was 50% Catholic Poles, 44% Jews (speaking Yiddish), 3% Lithuanians (Catholic?) and 1.5% Russian. The Lithuanians were hardly in town! Around that time, the whole country had 2 million people, of which 82% were Lithuanian and 8% Jewish. The Lithuanians (91%) were in the countryside, the Jews were in the towns (64%) and comprised most of the merchants (77%). And the Poles – of which 50% were illiterate – were in Vilnius? There was little mixing – less than 1% of Jewish marriages were "mixed."

How did they talk? What did they think of each other then? Clearly, the "language problem" is a very old one. In much of Europe, the children learn to speak 3-4 languages just from the street. There were separate schools, by government policy, until the Soviets required Russian in all of them, which means that the pre-Soviet state supported all these different schools and believed in letting them live their own way.

There were reforms about that time that gave land to peasants to farm but Jews were excluded. To qualify, the new farmers had to show that they knew how to farm, and Jews did not know how, typically. In 1882, Tsarist authorities even forbade Jews to live in the countryside and to engage in farming. That's why they ended up concentrated in the cities. On the other hand, the Polish authorities gave Jews seats in the constituent assembly proportional to population (6 out of 100). It seemed to be an environment of mutual respect, cultural separatism, and work according to who you are.

I just wish I knew who had which particular house. You know, when you see an old farm in the U.S., its provenance is usually known – the Jamisons lived there for three generations, and then it was sold to the Parkers. Which ended when they sold to farm to a townhouse or luxury house developer, but never mind. To the extent a home was in existence for a century, you might know what kind of people lived there. When you get into these European stone buildings that have survived more than five centuries, there can be more mixing of people in the house over time. When a neighborhood "went" to some undesirable group, it very likely "went" back at some point in the future. So, whether they wanted to or not, they shared a very intimate part of their lives.   Do you remember us drawing our fantasy pets in the bedroom closet? Or the mashed potatoes that splashed behind the refrigerator? Or the blood from my finger on the top of the window frame?

Still, I remember a friend lamenting that his gentry family's estate – taken over by Russian, then German, then Russian officers as quarters – was now a disco called "Estate Blues" in Polish. The new owners were exploiting the fascination for old times and the good life that had taken place in the huge building. There is probably a lot of that in Europe – castle chic, with the young mocking the ancient. Now the inhabitants are drunk and happy, listening to American pop sung with Polish, Lithuanian, and Russian accents, paying four times the going rate for a drink just to sit where the aristocracy had snoozed and schmoozed beside the fireplace.

Another dimension that I am groping with is literacy. When I think of America, I don't think of the country as being mostly poor illiterate peasants who rapidly got manipulated by the learned. I guess the American Indians were converted by Spanish missionaries, who brought them literacy along with God. But when you think of colonial America, you think of the drafters of the Constitution, not farmers. It must have been no different – class differences by literacy, if not by language, culture and religion. If you don't mix the kids in school, then you keep kids from falling in love across class lines. I guess in our mixed schools we pick up enough social cues to know if someone attractive is "appropriate." But what if you had to worry about whether the kid you had a crush on could *read*, never mind what college they went to or what religion they believed in?

I have to go back to the lab tonight, to check some cultures. Out of the past and the worries in my head; back to earth, for me, in the form of microorganisms, and the really simple life –
Zenius

Attachment: alleyofthecat.jpg

From: Mingen, Semea [semea@doos.com]
Sent: December 13, 2003
To: 'zen@ulink.net'
Subject: Re: mad cat

Zenius –

Thank you for remembering the fantasy pets in the closet. I had a meercat named "Cillian" and a ladybug named "Ionie." You had a dragon, and some dinosaurs. I lost sleep thinking your pets would eat mine. Finally, we drew the deepest ravine between them, into which the aggressors would fall if they tried to come over to my wall. When you were mad at me, you drew a fancy bridge over the ravine, and I would sneak in later and wash it away.

Semea

From: Mingen, Zenius [zen@ulink.net]
Sent: December 14, 2003
To: 'semea@doos.com'
Subject: drawing

Semea –

This morning on my dining table was a drawing that I attach a scan below. I have no idea where it came from! I can't believe someone got into my apartment! I don't know what to do – talk to police? Who would believe it could be so distressing to find a drawing? Would they believe me? They would probably guess I was drunk and left it there myself. Or had visitors who left it.

Help! What do you make of it?

Zenius

From: Mingen, Semea [semea@doos.com]
Sent: December 17, 2003
To: 'zen@ulink.net'
Subject: Re: drawing

Zenius –

The drawing is charming. Pretend you came across it at a sidewalk stall. Would you like it then? Can you pretend you got it that way, to make it less frightening? Tell me, really, do you ever have visitors to your apartment?

Are you getting Christmas invitations?

Take care, and calm down, Semea

From: Mingen, Zenius [zen@ulink.net]
Sent: December 20, 2003
To: 'semea@doos.com'
Subject: who owns the house

Semea –

It's been a week since the incident with the painting. I am trying to declare it a minor mystery and go on.

I read about an Africanist who thinks that all the problems in Africa are due to U.S. foreign policy. And, that the incidence of HIV/AIDS among blacks in the U.S. is the fault of racism. Blacks are just 12% of the population but 50% of the new AIDS cases. Black men are 9 times more likely to get AIDS than white men, and black women are 23 times more likely than white women. He suggests that "life style changes" can lower risk!! My problem with these scary sound bites is that they neglect to say whether economic status, age, family background, success in school, drug use, sexual preference, and sexual practices has anything to do with it. We are so bad at summarizing our problems. Maybe a "root cause" is that parents will not tell their children about sex, and scare the wits out of them early enough! Is this a universal – is there anywhere, besides the

South Sea Islands, where children learn how sex works as soon as they become interested? It really is as serious as teaching children not to drink poison, at this point.

Oh yes – the continuing story of "who really owns this house now?" Three brothers recently returned to a large farm in Poland that they claim was theirs 58 years ago, before World War II. It seems their family was originally German, and had long settled in Poland. After the war, they and about 13 million (?) others like them were forcibly expelled back to Germany. The Poles told all the Germans to get out, no matter that they had been part of the Polish landscape for generations. These brothers too felt they were victims of the war, even though their misfortune occurred immediately after. After the war, ethnic Germans still in Poland were killed, beaten, and raped, in retribution. Some men in the family fled from conscription into the Soviet Army in 1945, when the Russian's took charge, and some were killed by Polish soldiers for desertion from Polish forces. One day soon after the war, a Polish family came to the farm and claimed it, forcing them out.

The Polish who live on farms that had been "taken" from ethnic Germans now fear that with the entry to the European Union, more of these expelled Germans will return and claim their property. Or, they will return with their German wealth and buy up the lakes and forests. Currently, Germans cannot buy land in Poland, but Poles can buy land in Germany. The EU will equalize that.

The returning brothers were met with coffee and cake by the current owners of their family home, because the owners *really wanted to sell the property* and move to a resort town on the coast. They had not been able to find anyone willing to buy it! The current owners themselves were not really Poles, but Polish-Byelorussians expelled from Belarus by the Russians. So they were really "exiled or repatriated Poles." All of these expulsions were so common that restoration of property to former owners gets ridiculous. The claim from the visiting German brothers was ended amicably – they realized *they did not really want to live on a farm in a remote area of Poland*. They liked Germany pretty much. It would cost them to maintain ownership of the old homestead. It was a place no new buyers really wanted. Good sense overrode the sentimental urge to recover what had been lost.

Actually, I envy the German brothers. They were able to settle a spiritual and emotional score. It did not cost them very much – just a trip back to Poland. It lay to rest the endless conversations, every holiday gathering of family, of "woe is us – we was robbed." There are so many traumas of loss that are never settled, and cannot be settled by taking a trip, having a look and a conversation, and then feeling satisfied. I envy the sense of closure.

During World War I, 550,000 people were deported from Lithuania to Russia, including 160,000 (39%) Jews. After the war, 180,000 refugees returned from Russia. There must have been a lot of property changing hands!

I've been too busy to socialize much. Not up for holiday chatter anyway.

Zenius

From: Mingen, Semea [semea@doos.com]
Sent: December 28, 2003
To: 'zen@ulink.net'
Subject: Re: who owns the house

Zenius –

I think I have broken the code on the first drawing brought by the crow. The symbols are Lappish, or Sami – the northern tribes of Scandinavia. There is a Magician. A Boat of Death Reflecting in the Black Water On Which It Glides, Rotaimo the Kingdom of Death, and Bird Figures which symbolize the Playgrounds of the Birds on Nice Green Meadows Near Fishing Water. Oh yes, the red crayon suggests a sacred ghost (per theosophists anyway).

You are lucky I know a folk art expert.

Hope the winter is not too rough for you – Semea

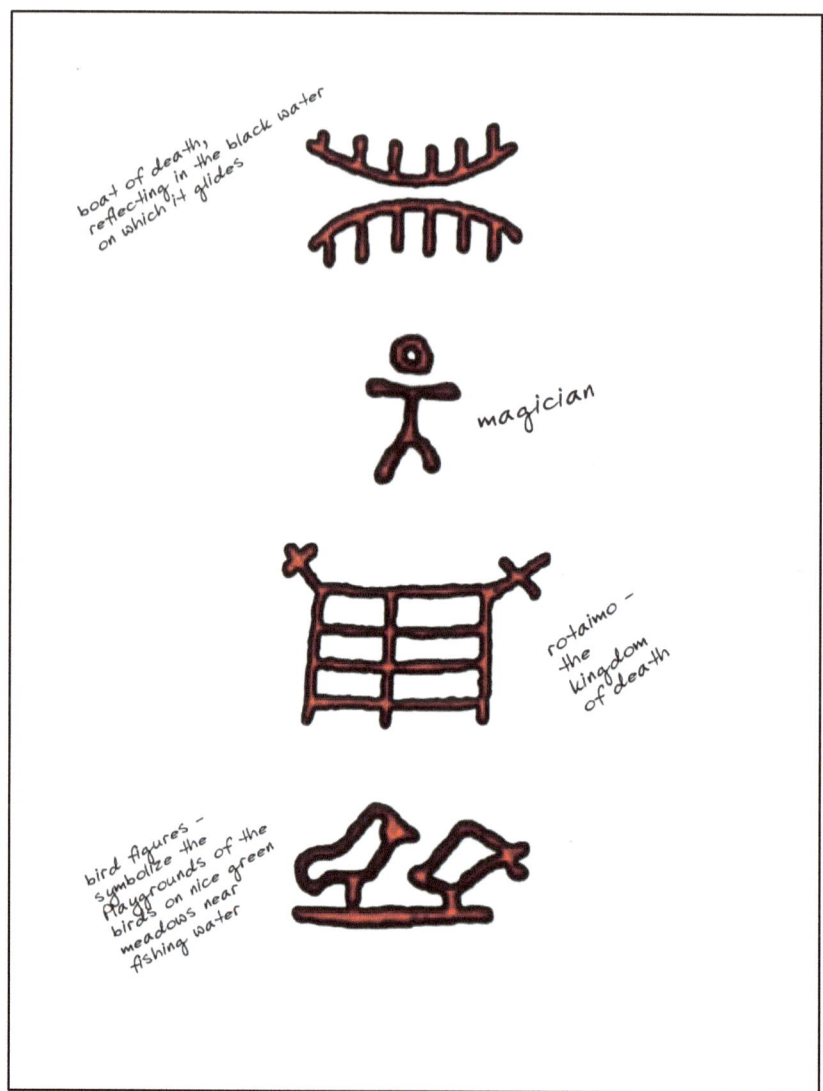

From: Mingen, Zenius [zen@ulink.net]
Sent: January 1, 2004
Priority: High
To: 'semea@doos.com'
Subject: eggs

Semea –

You won't believe what happened last night. I don't believe it. I am completely distracted. I came home after dark one night, and went into the kitchen for a beer, switched on the light, and saw broken raw eggs all over everything!! There had been a full carton in the fridge. Every one had been broken somewhere else – on the counter, on the table on the chair on the floor in the entry, on the coffee maker, down the front of the microwave. The empty carton was neatly put in the trash.

I checked the apartment to see if anything was missing. Couldn't find anything gone. Called up the landlord who lives out of town to ask what to do. He – Vincentas – asked if anything was missing? I said no, but what about the vandalism? He said forget it. Not worthy of attention. Just clean it up. Make sure you lock up. Check the windows.

Semea, the place WAS locked up. Someone would have had to have a key. But why come in just to do this?

It took two hours to clean up. I am so tired today. Worse than that, wondering who would do this? Why?

Zenius

From: Mingen, Semea [semea@doos.com]
Sent: January 3, 2004
To: 'zen@ulink.net'
Subject: Re: eggs

My dear Zeno –

I am so sorry. You are having some bad luck. It is unfair, for all the hard work you do.

Do something nice for someone today. And please get out of that laboratory and take in the air! Get some good energy somewhere. Even a good bowl of soup with friends. What about a bucket of hot salt water? I am sending you good thoughts.
Your sister Semea

From: Mingen, Zenius [zen@ulink.net]
Sent: January 10, 2004
To: 'semea@doos.com'
Subject: spiritual resistance

Semea –

Thanks for your sympathy last week. I tried to take your advice. Went out with Malke and had smoked fish and beer.

To take my mind off the research, I read about the "spiritual resistance" of Jews in Vilna ghetto. This book says that the leaders in the ghetto decided to fight the Nazis with their "spirit." They would deny the oppressor's view of them as victims, and rebel with dignity, hope, and self-worth. They would "fight torment with visible faith." "Sustain their humanity." So they organized the community – medical services, concerts, religious activities, sports. They held competitions in choral singing!

This is much like dancing on the Titanic. According to this book, they believed that they personally would escape destruction. The leader of the Jews, Yakov Gens, asked artists to organize performances to stimulate the will to live. I think this happened after only 15,000 were left, of 76,000 forced into the ghetto. Poetry readings, opera, prayers, piano, children's recitals. Gymnastics, boxing, tennis, basketball. Children dressed in white for a seyder snack. Gens stressed obedience, discipline, and work. "Work for life." Good German values – remember the Nazi death-camp sign "Arbeit Macht Frei."

Can you think of other times in history when people faced death with arts and crafts, and singing? And clubs. Many clubs. Even in the ghetto. Before the war, Jews were 13% of the population of Vilnius, but

60

they had 28% of the clubs and organizations in the town. (About 70,000 people, over 200 clubs.) The town was majority Polish by then (70%). I guess it was a minority's strategy for solidarity early in the century. It carried over into the ghetto.

Gens was asked by the Nazis to select groups of Jews for "special work details." For example, the Nazis would ask for 1,500. Finally both sides decided on 600. The Jewish Council had to prepare lists of those to be delivered, describe their occupation, age, etc, choose the place for the selection, organize it, find those in hiding, denounce them, and deliver them to the Nazis according to the prepared lists. All so organized! By both sides! Gens would send the Jewish ghetto police out to make the selection. They rounded up "the selected," who were transported out and killed. Gens thought that by giving up a small number, he was saving the majority. In Kovno, Rabbi Shapiro came to the same moral conclusion, after studying the holy texts – "give up the sick and elderly to save the majority." Of course it was hard to stay among the "well" as they were being starved.

And, at the same time, he discouraged any efforts for armed resistance by people in the ghetto. "Don't rock the boat, they'll kill us all." Which they did anyway.

The Nazis found out there was a small cadre planning to resist and demanded that the Judenrat – the Jewish Ghetto police -- give them up. Gens asked the ghetto community to take a vote and renounce the leader. The partisan leader, Vitenberg, surrendered, and was murdered by the Nazis. The partisans had no support from fellow Jews.

Truly like bargaining with the devil, except that Jews do not believe in a devil.

It is not as if they had no idea what happened to the batches of 500 or so people they gave up allegedly as laborers. Surviving children crawled out from under the bodies in the ditches at Panerai forest and found their way back to the ghetto, and told what happened. You can't ignore the massacre of 80,000. The ditches, by the way, had been dug for oil tanks, so they must have been very deep.

I cannot comprehend why they did not make weapons out of pots and pans instead of composing poetry and songs. What is it about our psyche that lets us dissociate from such profound horror?

Sorry to get caught up in these issues again, Semea. Mass death seems to be my issue.

By the way, thanks for deciphering the symbols. Yes, Kingdom of Death. I give up, still.

Zenius

From: Mingen, Semea [semea@doos.com]
Sent: January 20, 2004
To: 'zen@ulink.net'
Subject: Re: spiritual resistance

Zenius –

A curious thing happened the other day. We were at the art show at the Convention Center. I was with Don, Carrie, and Marjorie, having coffee. Marjorie was supposed to meet up with a date at this particular spot. She described him as having fantasy-good-looks. Lulu (4 years old) was in one of those huge play pens filled with foam balls. Sam, the date, walked up. He went over to Don and introduced himself and shook his hand. Lulu shouted that she wanted to shake his hand too, so she jumped out of the huge pen of balls in her socks and ran up to Sam. She shook his hand and asked to kiss him. He leaned down so she could reach his cheek. Carrie says Lulu has never done anything like that before!

Even odder is the fact that Lulu has declared that she is actually a boy from the time she could speak. She dresses as a prince or a cowboy on Halloween. She never wears dresses. When her parents introduce her as their daughter, she corrects them – "But I'm a boy!" I guess a dream date brought out the woman in her.

S.

From: Mingen, Zenius [zen@ulink.net]
Sent: January 25, 2003
To: 'semea@doos.com'
Subject: did we have the same parents?

Semea –

Sometimes I cannot believe we had nearly the same childhood. You are so different. We went to bed at the same time, ate cherries for the first time together, learned to fish together, sat eating sweet cantaloupe on a hike, heard the same loving words from our parents, and the scolds. All those same external experiences, and in your head, a different world. Wouldn't nearly the same genes make us nearly twins? I love you but I hardly know you. You say things that are odd, surprising. And then you laugh and I am home, and happy. I touch you like no other woman. An intimacy without sex. A love without the awful cycle of developing intimacy, then seeing it erode from ugly moments, the accumulation of small disappointments. Is romantic love programmed for failure? Do we have unrealistic hopes for it? I think because it is optional, where you, my sister are god-given forever, means we can arrive at a point of questioning romantic love, of letting it erode away, of letting someone else creep into our longings and lusts. And then one day we let it go or make ourselves let it go. Please don't divorce me, ever. I need a fixture of love to return to. My spiritual and emotional home. And don't go away, in any sense of the word. A very big part of me would die.

Love, Zenius

From: Mingen, Semea [semea@doos.com]
Sent: February 1, 2004
To: 'zen@ulink.net'
Subject: Re: did we have the same parents?

Zenius –

You place too much weight on statistics. You think that one million deaths are worth more than one. Zenius, one death can be your world.

Our life's lesson is exactly the experience of attachment and loss. You can experience it with a fly. Zenius, you keep looking for dimensions – statistics – to give something meaning. The meaning is in you! Do you grieve six million times for every Jew , or forty million times for every AIDS victim? It is a way to *de-personalize* death! Your "causes" are but detachments from personal feeling. You are dissociating, just like the Vilnius Jews in their "spiritual resistance."

I think Nisse calls to you. You have found 100 million ways to avoid feeling that.
With love, S.

From: Mingen, Zenius [zen@ulink.net]
Sent: February 15, 2004
To: 'semea@doos.com'
Subject: ...

Semea –

I remember her sleeping in my arms. Her young, beautiful skin, soft hair, sweet smell. She slept in my lap as if it were god's bed. Absolute comfort, loving bliss. And that's what I felt, holding her. She was life, my life, here and now. There is no replacement. No consolation. I feel dead and automatic now. The deep contentment she gave me is gone.

Lenore blamed me, even though neither of us was directly responsible. We taught her to stay away from electrical outlets, and blocked most of them. We taught her about fire and fast cars and heights and putting things in her mouth. Was it suicide, at age five? Semea, please explain to me how a child would do something completely out of character, like put a cord in her mouth? Semea, why?
Z.

From: Mingen, Semea [semea@doos.com]
Sent: February 21, 2004
To: 'zen@ulink.net'
Subject: Re: …

Zenius –
  You are sorry for yourself. Think of Nisse. She was done. She had a perfect life, which you gave her. Her soul chose it, lived it, and moved on. She chose new lives over seeing where her perfect child's life with you and Lenore would lead. She had given you pure love. You just don't feel like you got enough, and that is your lesson.
  She is teasing you, Zenius. Because you are being foolish and clinging to something she let go with that bolt of electric current.
  When did you last hear from Lenore?
S.

From: Mingen, Zenius [zen@ulink.net]
Sent: February 25, 2004
To: 'semea@doos.com'
Subject: devil

Semea –
  I woke up this morning and NEXT TO MY PILLOW was another drawing. I jumped out of bed and ran through the apartment, checking the door, the windows, the closets. I've been invaded. How can this be?
  I am going mad. This devil is undermining my sanity, my rationality. I cannot deny these episodes – there is physical evidence. I cannot explain them. Semea, tell me why THIS is happening to me. Do you know everything?
Z.

Attachment: drawing.jpg

From: Mingen, Semea [semea@doos.com]
Sent: February 29, 2004
To: 'zen@ulink.net'
Subject: Re: devil

Zenius –

Ask yourself why it is happening. You know. Purge all those statistics from your mind, and leave it open to truth that is not printed in the newspaper, a history book, a Nazi ledger, or a U.N. AIDS report.
S.

From: Mingen, Zenius [zen@ulink.net]
Sent: March 6, 2004
To: 'semea@doos.com'
Subject: Torah shoes

Semea –

In 1942, the Nazis appointed 20-40 Jewish intellectuals from the ghetto to select artifacts, books, and documents to preserve the culture. The things were piled in the YIVO Institute for Jewish Research. What actually happened? The books, manuscripts and papers ended up as waste paper in the local paper factory. Torah scrolls were sent off to be used to make shoes. About 20,000 of 100,000 books were sent to Frankfurt's Institute for Oriental Studies. Rare books were rescued by being smuggled into the ghetto, where they were hidden in cellars and such. I wonder if the shoes were marked in any way, and you could find them in some market stall? Torah shoes.

The drawings left in my house are baffling. They don't look like anything familiar – not people, animals, ships, storms, the seasons. I get nothing! Semea, make something of them!

I haven't heard from Lenore since we left the mediator's office two years ago. We signed the divorce agreement separately. She was so angry. All the discussions of retirement accounts, equity in the house, furniture she got from her mother, things we bought together, Nisse's toys and clothes – it is an old nightmare. I don't know why she turned on me so viciously. We were so happy, with Nisse. Did she blame me? I worked a lot, but I did not stop loving her. I think we could not cope together. She wanted something from me that wasn't there, and it was something she hadn't wanted before. Everything I did put her in a rage.

      The day Nisse died, she had marshmallows for breakfast. She looked out the window and saw clouds, and asked for marshmallows. Then she took each one and looked at it, and bit into it as if it were a chocolate truffle. She grinned, mostly to herself. I was reading a report and getting ready for a meeting that afternoon. She always played in the living room by herself. She played with dolls, and marbles, and beads, and little wind-up toys. She would chatter to herself, and laugh. I remember the silence that chilled me, and the cup of coffee that spilt as I pushed away from the table.

      Semea, tell me something happy.

Z.

From: Mingen, Semea [semea@doos.com]
Sent: March 13, 2004
To: 'zen@ulink.net'
Subject: Re: Torah shoes

Zeno –

      All meaning does not come in English sentences. I keep saying this. Open your mind. Humans have a common language. Have you seen the research on the fact that the same facial expressions convey the same emotions no matter what the tribe, language, religion, geography? We all recognize love, anger, dismay, sympathy, revulsion. Sanskrit aesthetics will tell you that all art evokes same small set of primal emotions.

      You are blocked on the idea that emotion is a communication. I think you are a victim of Western and male socialization. Your range is limited. You are not allowed to acknowledge or feel sadness, sympathy, or even love.

Zenius, imagine a world, and imagine a message, that engages those places forbidden to you – grief, love, simple joy, tenderness. You may use color, sound, motion. Try it without words.

I asked Adrian what was happening and he said it would do no good to tell you. (He didn't tell me either.)
S.

From: Mingen, Zenius [zen@ulink.net]
Sent: March 15, 2004
To: 'semea@doos.com'
Subject: three little birds

Semea –

We had some student helpers join us for a few weeks.

Helena of Finland wears the same scarf tightly over her hair every day. She has a long face with long cheeks and a small mouth. Small nose and eyes set high, and small oval glasses. She is short and walks with a shuffle, from the hips. She visits the kitchen a lot to eat a huge slather of Nutella on bread. She carries two recorders in her cloth bag, an alto and a soprano, and plays them or sings at every break. Her lips are almost pursed as if she cannot let much sound come out. She is a vegetarian. Very proficient in the lab, though. I try to imagine someone getting her drunk or having sex.

Goeteli of Belgium is a peach-plump cherub face and body. Wears a tank top and a skirt so that when she leans over, you can almost see her bottom. She looks like a Breugger painting. She sings like an angel and smiles and laughs freely. She has been to a number of student work camps in Europe and seems to be in the work camp groove.

Julia of Germany is petite with black hair and pale skin. Very feminine. Her full and frizzy hair is pulled back Reggae style with beads through it. She wears about 20 bracelets of different kinds – strings, beads, thin silver. She wears dark shirts and dark green shorts and something like Doc Martin shoes. One T-shirt has phrases in 10 languages. She is shy and stylized – like a German geisha. She and

Goeteli spontaneously started to use lots of gestures when they talk, giggling and pointing and waiving and then bursting out laughing. Totally contrary to cool women of the world. They are all about 19 years old.

I wish I could laugh the way they do! They remind me of Nisse, and of Lenore come to think of it. I might have been too serious for Lenore from the very start.

Z.

Attachment: julia.jpg

From: Mingen, Semea [semea@doos.com]
Sent: March 21, 2004
To: 'zen@ulink.net'
Subject: Re: three little birds

Zenius –

    Yesterday I looked out the window to the flagstone patio in the back yard two stories below. It was early on a sunny morning. There were two doves side by side, collapsed against the flagstone, snuggling it. There were clearly together and moved around but stayed facing each other. It was like an early morning sun bath, sensual, feathery, extremely affectionate. I could not hear them coo. They were having a moment. Not directly sex. Just intense bird love.

    I am watching a dwarf willow tree in my yard open its pussy-willow buds. They wait for just the right temperature and the right angle of the sun, in the spring, then one by one wake up. They are fuzzy gray-white things, surprisingly insistent, pushing back the protective casing that hardened from all the battering cold. Each one bumps its way out alone, and discovers that just two inches away, another sibling has appeared. They are on the way of being one of thousands, dancing in the spring wind, on vine-like branches. They'll get bigger and fuzzier. And unlike fruit buds, the birds will leave them alone. Just lucky, in the turn they got.

S.

From: Mingen, Zenius [zen@ulink.net]
Sent: March 27, 2004
To: 'semea@doos.com'
Subject: escape

Semea –

    An American called Zalys Gintalas came by. Imagine how people in the U.S. spelled his name. He heard I was here and wanted to talk. He grew up in Chicago, going to Saturday language schools, Catholic Church, summer youth camp, holiday parties. He is here traveling with his elderly mother who wanted one last journey before her strength was gone.

Zalys told me that at the turn of the 20ᵗʰ Century, nearly 400,000 Lithuanians emigrated to America – 25% of the population, due to economic hardship and Russian conscription. In the U.S., they became industrial workers. They became rich and urbanized and organized into close ethnic communities. Of course it took a generation for the first immigrants to graduate from living four, five, and six to a room. In 1914, more than half lived four to a room, and about a tenth lived six to a room. They took advantage of education, set up churches, community centers, and newspapers – at least 225 papers in the early 1900's. There were more Lithuanian newspapers in the U.S. than in Lithuania, where tsarist censorship was in effect. The majority of the people living back home were in the countryside, and working farms, if they were not deported or returning from deportation to Russia. There are nearly a million Lithuanian-Americans now, where the homeland has 3.5 million. And there are long traditions of the richer émigrés investing in businesses and helping back home, even influencing politics.

I guess you and I did not grow up that way. It is a strange relationship to the U.S., in my mind. When does an immigrant become an American? What's the balance between clinging to a romanticized world of the past and participating in the welcoming land of plenty? Now that I read about all these dislocations of masses of people, constantly, it seems that national identity is very artificial. However, when the hostilities rise, then everyone seems to know who is what, and hold them to it, and even kill them for it.

At the end of the War, when our parents were in refugee camps, there were 7 million people "liberated" at the time. There were nearly 60,000 Lithuanians exiled in the three Allied occupied zones. A fourth of them were children. They were watched and screened, and restricted, as the Allies tried to ferret out Nazi collaborators. Our parents were among 227 priests, 130 seminarians, 400 engineers, 300 physicians, 350 lawyers, 60% of the membership of the Lithuanian Writer's Association, 400 people from Kaunas and Vilnius universities, 300 primary school teachers, 700 high school teachers, and 200 other teachers. The refugee camps had 4000 students, with 14 junior high and 20 high schools, employing 1000 teachers. Nearly a whole town of professionals and leaders and writers "displaced," and ready to move on, hopefully away from the new Soviet occupation. The Soviets, of course, wanted them back. Probably to fill their empty deportation camps. These were exactly like our parents on the "death lists."

The U.S. passed a Displaced Persons Act in 1948. England wanted women to work in hospitals and sanitariums. The Belgians wanted coal miners. Canada wanted men to clear forests and build roads. 30,000 Lits were poured into the U.S.

All over the world, neighbors rise up against each other. How could so many normal people engage in genocide of their neighbors? I mean to read a book by Richard Rhodes who has an explanation of the Nazis. Nazis found it hard to get people with college degrees to engage in cold blooded murder so they developed gas chambers – they industrialized the killing to depersonalize it. That way, professionals could look at the "killing machine" as a tool, and get caught up with the need to develop it, operate it, and improve it. Apparently they kept very good records on their "industry" – good models for operations research and management information systems.

I am truly grateful our parents escaped, although they lost a lot by it too. Is there something in the air dragging me into these issues? Sorry –
Z.

From: Mingen, Semea [semea@doos.com]
Sent: April 2, 2004
To: 'zen@ulink.net'
Subject: Re: escape

Zenius –
Tulips have just arrived in the markets. The early ones come from Mexico. Can you picture that the new "blond Dutch girls in wooden shoes" walking through fields of tulips are now possibly short, dark girls wearing light cotton dresses and sandals? I guess flowers get stereotyped too – hibiscus and orchids from Hawaii, sunflowers from the South, tulips and Holland. Of course, the colors go with Mexican folk art and make a lot of sense there – solid white, red, purple, yellow. For Holland, tulips seem a

happy moment after a long rainy winter, an expression of fantasy in a normally subdued, Europe-tasteful and tame existence. Did I get my stereotype from those old master paintings? In Mexico, they would blend with clothes, paintings, festivals already a riot of color. Why didn't the Mexicans grow tulips before? Maybe they did and we didn't know it.

I bought a bundle because somehow a huge pile of tulips, leaning out of a vase, is the picture of sensuality and opulence to me. Maybe I got imprinted looking at old paintings, where the feathery mound of a dead pheasant, and apples and pears, are right there with the mounds of tulips. I wish tulips had found a painter like Van Gogh – someone who just lost himself in their color and shape. I just don't get the same feeling from carnations, for example, or geraniums. Tulips are regal. Large, giant tissue petals that kiss the air.

I hope you see lots of spring flowers soon.
Love, Semea

From:	Mingen, Zenius [zen@ulink.net]
Sent:	April 12, 2004
To:	'semea@doos.com'
Subject:	disaster

Semea –

AGAIN!!! I raced to a meeting today, at the Baltic Regional Scientific Coordination Center on HIV/AIDS. It was pouring rain. Wet slippery cobble stones. Cars driving slowly. Lots of umbrellas trying to pass each other on three-foot sidewalks. I finally got to the meeting, pulled out my folder of documents, and found a drawing instead! My colleagues thought I was crazy – I was angry and just flummoxed. Semea, what is this? What is happening to me? Can you ask your psychic? I don't think I can find a detective here, at least not someone who did not work for the KGB before. I cannot concentrate. I cannot work like this. Do I need a psychiatrist?
Z.

Attachment: thing.jpg

From: Mingen, Zenius [zen@ulink.net]
Sent: April 18, 2004
To: 'semea@doos.com'
Subject: the health gap

Semea –

There is a new report on TB from the World Health Organization. TB is killing more people due to AIDS – a compounding effect. About a third of the world has the TB bacterium but have immune systems that can contain it. With AIDS, it is flourishing again – 8.8 million people developing it each year. It can be cured in six months with drugs that cost $10, but that assumes it is detected, and that the patient takes the drugs. As with AIDS, women are more likely to get TB, because they are twice as likely to get AIDS in Africa. Semea, in the worst country it is 16 times more prevalent that in the U.S. Our major gap used to be the rich and the poor, the industrialized versus the underdeveloped – now it is the decimated-by-disease versus the healthy. Do we really believe it will stay on the African continent? That our medicines will immunize us? Globalization means sharing this horror.

By the way, China is finally getting over their denial about sexual activity. As young people adopt our ways (early premarital sex, multiple partners) the rates of disease are going up. Since they have 1.3 billion people (more than 4 times America) their trends are magnified. For example, they could get to Africa's rate of infection of 20% (and 40% in some countries), which is roughly 260 million people. Unfortunately, their response is vastly slower. Another disaster on its way. Is this the plague of the 21ˢᵗ Century? We are watching 30 million people die now. Will our world population be "corrected"? By how much?

The three teens talked me into joining them for a trip to Grautas Park. Took 2 hours by bus. A "mushroom millionaire" bought up old statues of Lenin, Stalin, Marx, and other stars of the communist era. He bought up a beautiful forest setting and built about 2 miles of boardwalk going from one statue to the next. Some are more than 20 feet tall. Remember Saddam Hussein being pulled down – "mega" size. Each statue has a fact sheet in Lithuanian, Russian, and English, explaining who this is and what he did. Many of them were very bad boys, deporting thousands, big massacres, secret police and torture. The "park of infamy" has a surreal feel. Looks the usual "celebration of our heroes." But there are a few watch towers in the woods and a rustic forest camp mock-up to remind us of the bad days. The millionaire – who had some direct experience – wanted visitors to get to the park riding a packed cattle car, to simulate deportations, but there was a great controversy about the whole thing ("too grim" "over the top"), and he compromised.

Some locals say it is too depressing to go to this park. Feels like climbing back into a spiritual death ditch. It occurred to me that the twin towers site in NYC is like hundreds of places here. Bare, fresh reminders of large-scale murder. Except there are many, many more here. There is a wall in the synagogue listing 140 TOWNS that don't exist any more. A beautiful, renovated old building smack in the middle of the old town has a plaque on it: "This was the synagogue inside the Vilnius ghetto." The grand building is now the Austrian embassy.

I went for a walk in Rasu Cemetery. It is full of Polish and Lithuanian and some Russian names. Everybody sharing the same dirt. After death, no more fighting, or genocide, or deporting each other, or taking over your neighbor's house and using their fine dishes and linens, no more hiding in closets and under floor boards, no more cowering and cringing and fearing every person you pass, and having your youth robbed, or your babies smashed, or your health ruined for life. Peace. Z.

Attachment: rasuangel.jpg

From: Mingen, Semea [semea@doos.com]
Sent: April 20, 2004
Priority: High
To: 'zen@ulink.net'
Subject: Re: the health gap

Zenius –

Are you suicidal? I think you should see a psychiatrist. Please come back. You are not sounding like a scientist, or a humanist. You are sounding depressed. Would you like me to visit?
Your sister Semea.

From: Mingen, Zenius [zen@ulink.net]
Sent: April 24, 2004
To: 'semea@doos.com'
Subject: not yet

Semea –

Not yet. Not yet. Not yet.

I just read "Muppets With a Message of Hope" in Newsweek, about a muppet educating African children about HIV. In the U.S., TV can reach 800 million people in six months – two thirds of the world's television viewers. Will a Muppet get people to stop what they are doing?

Did you know that a black man in America is nine times more likely to get the disease than a white man, and a black woman 23 times more likely than a white woman? This is ethnic self-destruction more insidious than genocide, because there is no one to blame. There are people in China who have never heard of AIDS, and 40% (of 1.3 billion!) do not know you can prevent it. It is incomprehensible to me that we cling to ignorance, stigmas, discrimination to the point that simple facts – sex can kill you – cannot get through. Maybe if we made Godzilla movies with AIDS as the monster, everyone would get it. Godzilla does not have sex though. It is easier to understand the destruction of a fantasy monster than the invisible transmission of a virus.

I must say a big change is in international cooperation. Here is one for you: UNAIDS Reference Group on Estimates, Modelling and Projections. Statistics may indeed cure us. The Baltics are showing five-fold increases in AIDS over a few years. If AIDS were an intentional human agent, it would be deemed very successful indeed. Trending up fantastically!

The three girls in the lab dragged me to a free concert. An Estonian group called Alle-aa. Their music is very authentic – "runic." Some call and response type songs. Simple instruments like Appalachian folkies might have. A little melancholy. Apparently as old as a century Before Christ. (And the melancholy still resonates!) We were in the park, with a warm sun, slight breeze. A bunch of eight teenagers passed us, the whole row arm in arm, singing "Summertime." I cannot imagine American teens being that uninhibited, unless they were drunk.

You'll be proud of me. Yesterday I came home to another incident. I brought a bunch of bright sticky notes on this trip to mark up reports and such, thinking I might not get them here. They were all over my apartment. Color-coded trails of them through the rooms, up the walls, around pictures, up and over the dresser, like flags for organized ants to follow. Must have used up 500 stickers. The orange path and the neon green path and the neon yellow path. They all ended up at a closet. Inside the closet door, where my clothes had been pulled off hangers and dropped to the floor, and on the back of the closet was another drawing. It took me an hour to pick up all the stickers. I am resigned.
Still sort of o.k. – Z.

Attachment: stickup.jpg

From: Mingen, Semea [semea@doos.com]
Sent: April 30, 2004
To: 'zen@ulink.net'
Subject: Re: not yet

Zenius –

Have you heard of poltergeist? It is ghost that is called up by your own emotions and energies. It personifies some turmoil inside of you, but takes on its own "life." You are energizing it.

The folk music sounds interesting. You know that early slave music in America had roots in African call and response songs. Communal singing is never going to get old. Here's a favorite shape-note song called Africa C.M. by William Billings:

Now shall my inward joys arise,
And burst into a song;
Almighty love inspires my heart,
And pleasure tunes my tongue.
...
Why do we then indulge our fears,
Suspicions and complaints?
Is He a God, and shall His grace
Grow weary of His saints?

Ideally it is nearly screamed by a large group of people divided by voice into four quadrants facing each other. No instruments needed! (You'll recognize Amazing Grace from this genre, and that song is really called New Britain.)
Semea

From: Mingen, Zenius [zen@ulink.net]
Sent: May 3, 2004
To: 'semea@doos.com'
Subject: catacombs

Semea –

Goeteli, Helena and Julia dragged me to a night club. We had to walk down into catacombs of ancient stone, going through a series of small rooms, ducking under thick arches of rock. It seemed odd to go by a pool table and look into corners of what seemed like the basement of a castle. Renovation is out of the question, of course. The mostly young people just pour themselves into the space and order a beer. In the U.S. this would be a national treasure, roped off for precious limited viewing and photographs during the day only. Here, we just lean against the indestructible stone walls and hang into the night. It does not help to be claustrophobic, however. And service means waiting for the occasional appearance of someone who peeks into your space, because they may be roaming a large underground. Ventilation is iffy, also. I am sure no one has checked oxygen levels. The three of them were carefree, breaking into snippets of songs they have taught each other. Finnish teen folk.

Lit natives are not unhappy. They are exuberant about the arrival of endless possibility. They can imagine driving out of the country for a vacation. Foreigners are flooding the streets. New businesses and hotels popping up. Signs saying Arthur Anderson, IBM, travel, imports, Holiday Inn. This opening world feels very creative, and experimental. I have had the feeling, on the street, of both "we've been left out and we are behind" but also strongly "anything is possible." A mix of old and new that I saw in India. Collision of people who want to take it slow and people who want to start everything from scratch and right away. Being post-Soviet occupied must be a little like arriving as a refugee in your own country. Who were we when we lived our own lives? What do we have left to work with now?

The scary things are seeing old retired people begging a post office clerk not to cut off their pension payment. They are nearly starving *with* the pension. The bureaucratic clerk is rude, indifferent, tired. The retiree has no feeling of entitlement and security. I imagine the government support seems callous, whimsical, and arbitrary – in the hands of a cranky old-style clerk. (Or is that an image from fiction?) I do see old women begging on the streets. They are wearing layers of cotton clothes, and usually a head scarf (village style?). I wonder where they go at night.

Zenius

From: Mingen, Semea [semea@doos.com]
Sent: May 7, 2004
To: 'zen@ulink.net'
Subject: Re: catacombs

Zenius –

I put up three hanging flower planters on the porch. Put a mixture of violets, lush purple and blazing white, and delicate blue and white flowers. High up, just under the eaves. A sparrow took to visiting the one on the end, clearly building a nest. Over several days, she flew in and out, in and out, hundreds of trips. I forgot to pay attention to her, except one day I went out to read on the porch and she screeched at me nearly the whole time, trying to harass me away. I watered the plants, reaching way over my head with a watering can, aiming at the outer edges of the planter so as to cover all the 4-5 plants in the pot.

One day I lifted the pot down, and there was a neat nest with two scrawny, hairy lumps in it. I completely missed the egg stage. They looked like something the cat coughed up, mucousy, half-digested tiny creatures. They were fast asleep. I had to water very carefully after that.

They got more feathers and clear baby beaks. They were always asleep and squashed against each other, like conjoined twins. Only once did an eye open and peek at the monster with the giant watering can.

One day, they were gone.

I found another shape-note song for you called Thomas Town:

Great God how frail a thing is man,
How swift his minutes pass.
His age contracts within a span,
He blooms and dies like grass.

(Remember Brahms' Requiem – "all flesh is like grass"?) Semea

From:	Mingen, Zenius [zen@ulink.net]
Sent:	May 14, 2004
To:	'semea@doos.com'
Subject:	results

Semea –

We've made progress on the vaccine. That does not mean the final answer, but our piece of testing whether a certain drug induces responses related to defenses is promising. We are reporting to the HIV Vaccine Trials Network and planning to give a paper at the meetings in three months. We are pretty excited to have promising results.

I have been very absorbed in analyzing the data. Ten hour days, dark walks home. Grabbing soup and bread or apple crepes on the way. The weather is still fairly decent, although it is cooler. Have to remember to bring a jacket for the night return.

Speaking of clothes. Last week I got home at ten p.m. and found ALL my clothes lay out on the bed, neatly, overlapping in a large mound, layer by layer. You know how Middle-Eastern rug merchants will throw out one rug at a time, on top of the prior ones, so you can get a good look at it? Same thing, only these were my shirts and pants and sweaters, coats, underwear, ties, hats. And at the bottom of the pile, which took an hour to reach as I put everything away, was another drawing!

The girl troika is taking me to a performance of Carmina Burana next week. I feel like a special project. They flirt a little bit, but most of their attention is on the students at the university nearby. They are constantly looking for fun and mixing. I have no idea how much of that is carnal.

They told me they went into a restaurant where there is a phone on every table. The phone rang right away. They were taken for prostitutes and got a generous offer, which they laughed off.
Z.

Attachment: atbottom.jpg

From: Mingen, Semea [semea@doos.com]
Sent: May 16, 2004
To: 'zen@ulink.net'
Subject: Re: results

Zenius –

When you hear Carmina, please pay attention.
There is a snippet from **Ego sum abbas**:

Wafna, wafna!	Ow! Ow!
Uid fecisti sors turpassi	Awful Fate, what have you done?
Nostre vite gaudia	You have taken away
Abstulisti omnia!	all the joys of my life!

S.

From: Mingen, Zenius [zen@ulink.net]
Sent: May 20, 2004
To: 'semea@doos.com'
Subject: a real pagan

Semea –

I met an actual pagan. You know god is "dievas" which has the same root as the Hindu "divas." (Indo-European.) The pagan's most important sanctuary is in Prussia, where dad grew up. Malke says there are millions of pagans now. A well-known Lithuanian archaeologist, Marija Gimbutas, had a pagan burial in 1994. Although Christianity came in the late 14ᵗʰ century, it stayed in rural areas long into the 18ᵗʰ century when Lithuanian was indeed almost totally agrarian. Malke says there are about 200 in a core group now. The Hill of Crosses for example is a symbol of Catholic resistance to the Soviets. But it was said to be a sacred pagan mound originally. Now the pagans claim they are being held in contempt by the Catholics. I asked Malke what do they actually do. He says they have gatherings at sites in the forest and sing old hymns and retell mythological stories. They have sacred serpents, gods of thunder, legends of the iron wolf, charms, and fire.   Maybe robes, but I am guessing.

I told Malke about the mischief in my house. He laughed and said, "Don't be surprised! Look where you are." (?) As if there were more spirits in Vilnius that anywhere else. Kind of a pagan's boast.

I am finally taking a page from your book. Wrote another note to put in the carved wooden "dark angel." This one says "Answer me!"

Two days ago when I got back to my apartment all the water faucets were on.

Later, Z.

From: Mingen, Semea [semea@doos.com]
Sent: May 22, 2004
To: 'zen@ulink.net'
Subject: Re: a real pagan

Zenius –

We went on hike up at Mount Baker this time. I like to visit the hot springs that are scattered all over the back woods. There was a clear trail to this spot, and, unfortunately, it is not a secret. We hiked about 1.5 hours up through forest to get to it. There were several creeks along the way. Nice path, rich pines. In a clearing was a pool of water. There were a few people in it. Protocol on these things is "clothing optional." Gary, Susan, Darla and I went around to the farthest side from the incumbents – about 30 feet away. Stripped and got in. It is delightful – if not pagan – to abandon civilization in the forest. With no oppressors either! Maybe some shy people.

S.

From: Mingen, Zenius [zen@ulink.net]
Sent: May 26, 2004
To: 'semea@doos.com'
Subject: making people disappear

Semea –

I read that the Stalinists put away 18 million people in the Gulag and far North between 1929 and 1953. That is a very high number. People were terrorized into silence. They cowered and watched people get picked up and hauled away at night. It was not an industrialized killing system like the Nazis, but had to be a very elaborate deportation and transport system. Imagine setting up camps for 18 million!! One authority says the Gulag was the single largest employer in the world and yet it never managed to pay for itself.

Our parents were still in Vilnius when the Soviet deportations of 1941 took place. About 40,000 people deemed "socially harmful" were taken with 20 minutes or sometimes a day's notice. They were merchants, business people, land owners, Polish military, Roman Catholic leaders, Jewish leaders, and homeless and prostitutes. They thought the trains were going to Kazakhstan. Sometimes the journey included a forced march of days without food or water. Some drank their urine or blood due to extreme thirst. They were shot if they fell down. The testimonials on the web list individuals, and detailed stories, with the names of the local police who helped.

One of the functions of the Gulag system was to provide slave labor to the state. There is research on the economic value of slaves in the U.S. In the 1850's, the price was about $3,500 apiece. About ten years later it was more than one million dollars. So something like 10 million slave laborers around 1940 had to be worth millions each to somebody. Too bad that did not show in the economic growth of the Soviet Union. I think a lot were just busting rocks and dying, rather than working factories.

This past week I got home to find all my books thrown under the bed. It was very hard to get them out – using the broom. Included among them of course was another drawing. I am really dreading my own apartment door these days. I am so tired of this!
Z.

Attachment: wbooks.jpg

From: Mingen, Semea [semea@doos.com]
Sent: June 1, 2004
To: 'zen@ulink.net'
Subject: Re: making people disappear

Zenius –

I got a phone call from Lenore this week. She wanted to know if I had any photos of Nisse. She says you destroyed all the photos in the house, and she was hoping I had some. Did you really? Why?

She was very cordial, and subdued. I don't know why you two fell out so badly. You had such a paradise going there. You'll have to explain it to me some day.

S.

From: Mingen, Zenius [zen@ulink.net]
Sent: June 7, 2004
To: 'semea@doos.com'
Subject: earth to angel

Semea –

I am having a bad spell. Overslept yesterday because my alarm clock was off. Curiously, the night before, when I got into bed, the bed was warm. I was too tired to think about it then. I am getting coughing fits, like an allergy or something. Very disruptive in meetings. Actually have to get up and leave the room and double over out in the hall. I cannot seem to find what triggers it, outdoors or indoors.

I put another note in the dark angel. This one says: "Tell me." How's that for spiritual progress?

Work was particularly bad because some data I had been keeping in notebooks got misplaced. I went through everything in the lab and at home to find it. So tedious. Finally it turned up – days later – in a drawer that I thought I had checked. The tension was high and I tried to hide it from the others, but they knew I was "off."

Oh, I am attaching my "Gulag image" – a photo of a wood carving I took out in the boonies. Pagan? Modern? I think it is a modern version

of the Rupintojelis, the traditional "pensive or grieving Christ" that is a national icon. The wood carvings are all over the countryside, I'm told, and, many artists do one in their style. A pensive Christ, instead of a crucified Christ. Curious emphasis. I'll let you analyze that.
Z.

Attachment: closesadguy.jpg

Attachment: sadguy.jpg

From: Mingen, Semea [semea@doos.com]
Sent: June 12, 2004
To: 'zen@ulink.net'
Subject: Re: tell me

Zenius –

This week I went to visit my friends Donna and Bill who have a small farm. They have a new foal, jet black, frisky. It just leaps and runs like crazy around the pasture when they let it loose. Like at two year old that's been sitting in a car for hours. Only much bigger, and heavier, and stronger. A very BIG toddler. Can knock things down, including people. We are so used to cute small baby animals that we forget there are very large babies out there too, and they don't know we are fragile.

S.

From: Mingen, Zenius [zen@ulink.net]
Sent: June 21, 2004
To: 'semea@doos.com'
Subject: love bite

Semea -

I woke up with a big boil on my neck. Malke says, what's that, a love bite? It is embarrassing. I am wearing high collars. The coughing continues. It occurred to me that I am working with a virus. We have very little of the virus in the lab, and it is fairly protected, but you never know. I wonder if I came in contact some how? I keep thinking about it, all day. Can't sleep. It is warm outside, but I feel lousy. Chilled. Had to buy a turtleneck with a high collar. Try not to look diseased when I tried it on.

My colleagues are starting to avoid me. Fewer lunches, or late night shooting the breeze. Maybe I have bags under my eyes. It's true I haven't done much besides work so I might be getting one-dimensional. They used to like explaining customs to me, and telling me about their families.

Also, I had another big start. A drawing turned up taped to the lamp on my desk. Clearly intended for me. A strange object in a lab, so colorful. My colleagues – except for Malke – have no idea that there is a history to this. They just thought a visitor dropped by and left it. Although nobody saw anyone. It threw me off, because I felt safe from that surprise at work. This is like being teased by a terrorist, who hasn't threatened to harm me, yet, but still plays these games.

Z.

Attachment: ondesk.jpg

From:	Mingen, Zenius [zen@ulink.net]
Sent:	June 26, 2004
To:	'semea@doos.com'
Subject:	test

Semea –

I have been feeling awful and asked around about doctors. I got an AIDS test. The results were ambiguous. Can you believe that? I don't know what to think. Did they get it wrong? Do I need to get another one? The boil on my neck has a hard feel to it. Really obvious now, and repulsive. I am working hard and too tired to take the time off. Have to work to concentrate. We are close to the end of our project. Everybody working a part of it. I don't feel I can slack off now.

Sorry I am too tired to write much – Z.

From:	Mingen, Zenius [zen@ulink.net]
Sent:	July 6, 2004
To:	'semea@doos.com'
Subject:	freak

Semea –

A terrible thing happened. There was a freak accident in the lab. About once a week each one of us is supposed to check the refrigerators and incubators. It is routine. Somehow the incubators were turned off, and the cultures were ruined. Everyone knew it was my turn. They asked me what happened. I think someone else pushed the switch, maybe by accident, because I have never made that mistake. It just doesn't seem real. There was a confrontation. Malke tried to defend me, but the others were really heated about it. It is a devastating set-back. We are all at a loss. It means a month of work to recover. Someone said maybe I wanted to prolong my trip. I was really angry to hear that – as if I needed to resort to that to get more time! I haven't done anything to deserve that! I'll be working really hard to repair the situation.

By the way, in my briefcase, the attached...   Z.

Attachment: surprise.jpg

From: Mingen, Semea [semea@doos.com]
Sent: July 9, 2004
To: 'zen@ulink.net'
Subject: Re: freak

Zenius –
        You don't say if you've seen a doctor. I wish you would! You've got to take care of yourself first. Please!
S.

p.s. I mailed you something.

From: Mingen, Semea [semea@doos.com]
Sent: July 23, 2004
Priority: High
To: 'zen@ulink.net'
Subject: HELLO

Zenius –
        Are you there? Are you well? I tried to call the lab but there was no answer. No answering machine. I wish I knew your friend Malke's address. I thought of calling the Consulate but then held off in case it would embarrass you. PLEASE DROP ME A NOTE! I AM WORRIED.
S.

From: Mingen, Semea [semea@doos.com]
Sent: August 7, 2004
Priority: High
To: 'zen@ulink.net'
Subject: OK?

Zenius –
       I am calling the Consulate if you don't respond in two days. If you
can get to a phone, please call me. PLEASE!
S.

From: Mingen, Zenius [zen@ulink.net]
Sent: August 9, 2004
To: 'semea@doos.com'
Subject: Rasu

Semea –

I am sorry to be out of touch so long. I am finally better.

When I got your envelope I was feverish, stuck at home with nausea and weakness. The situation at work got worse. They asked me to stay home for a week to settle things down. On my way home I bought some Suktinis – the mead that has about 15% ethyl alcohol. I thought I would see if I could burn out the awful feeling in me.

I started drinking. It was a clear summer night. I made my way to the Rasu Cemetery again. A very atmospheric place with ancient overgrown headstones. It is very hilly and has lots of places to hide. Lots of places to crawl into, if necessary. Tombstones of all shapes and sizes, like trees on a hill.

After some drunken meditation, I remembered the envelope from you and opened it, and there was Nisse. The picture just fried my heart. I could hardly bear it. The cold of the cemetery and the heat of the Suktinis, and the agony of remembering her. My personal Gulag.

I was there all night. Not twenty years in the Gulag, but a soul-sucking experience.

When I got home and took a shower, I noticed the bump on my neck had opened. Believe it or not, a thing was coming out. Fortunately it only took about an hour. Totally disgusting, invasive, parasitical, gruesome, dumb, and alive. I took it to a doctor and he said I might have picked it up in India. It could have taken a year to grow and find a way out. It looked – you'll laugh – like the AIDS virus does under a microscope.

I am certified well again. I am packing up to leave next week. Back to Portland. I'll call you then.

I had never seen that photo of Nisse before. By the way, she liked to break eggs. She liked colored stickers, and running the faucet, and going through my closet. I forgot.

Love, Zenius

From: Mingen, Semea [semea@doos.com]
Sent: August 9, 2004
To: 'zen@ulink.net'
Subject: Re: Rasu

Zenius –

Thank God.   Here's some Carmina.

Veris leta facies   (The merry face of spring)

Cytharizat cantico	Like a harp sings
Dulcis Philomena,	the sweet nightingale,
Flore rident vario	with many flowers
Prata iam serena,	the joyous meadows are laughing,
Salit cetus avium	A flock of birds rises up
Silve per amena,	through the nice forest,
Chorus promit virgin	a chorus of girls
Iam gaudia millena.	Now promises a thousand joys.

Ecce gratum   (Oh, sweet spring)

Iamiam cedant tristia!	Sadness is gone!
Estas redit,	Summer is back,
Nunc recedit	now recedes
Hyemis sevitia.	the severity of winter.
…	
Illi mens est misera,	He is wretched
Qui nec vivit,	who does not live
Nec lascivit	or love
Sub Estatis dextera.	by summer's rules.

Love, Semea

Attachment: nisse.jpg

www.ingramcontent.com/pod-product-compliance
Lightning Source LLC
Chambersburg PA
CBHW041408010726
47507CB00001B/40